REACTION

re-ac-tion

/rē akSH(ə)n/

*An action performed or a feeling experienced
in response to a situation or event*

For EILEEN — ENJOY!

[signature]

IAN K. KENT

Tellwell Talent
www.tellwell.ca

ISBN
978-0-2288-2131-1 (Paperback)
978-0-2288-2132-8 (eBook)

DEDICATION

This is for my wonderful son, Danny. When he was a boy, I first showed him some of the exciting things about marine life and coastal sailing. Years later, as an internationally respected Marine Biologist, he described to me some fascinating facts about the natural poisons of *Tetrodotoxin* from a fish, and *Batrachotoxin*, from poison dart frogs, *Phyllobates terribilus*. These facts triggered some of the ideas in this story.

CHAPTER 1

When Dr. Heinrich Kohler got out of bed Wednesday morning, he had no idea it was the last morning he would ever see. Being an early riser, Kohler normally started his morning with a five to ten kilometre run before breakfast. He considered it good medicine for brain and body. This day was especially important, as he was scheduled to present one of the most important and controversial papers of his career at the International Environmental Conference on Global Warming in Vancouver, Canada.

Booked into a comfortable downtown hotel, he had arrived from his native Austria on the previous weekend. His early arrival provided a few extra days to help overcome jet-lag and provide enough time to visit some friends before the conference. Normally, he would be up by dawn, slip on his track suit, take his iPod and a bottle of mineral water and head out of the hotel for his before breakfast run. The past few mornings he had enjoyed exceptional weather, incredible scenery and also had met another runner doing the same run, so he left his iPod in the room. Vancouver was ideal for this activity, and the hotel where he was staying was close to the famous Stanley Park and its "seawall" path. At one thousand acres, Stanley Park is one of the largest urban parks in North America, and offers a variety of walking paths, small lakes, wildlife and other attractions for nature lovers. Ringing the park at just above sea level is the seawall, a well developed five-and-a-half-mile path for walkers, joggers and cyclists. Time permitting, a serious runner could cover the entire length of the seawall at one run. After walking the entire seawall on Sunday, Heinrich had decided to split the run into two sections so each day he could alternate, providing an ample run without taking too much time. After returning to the hotel, he would shower, change and head down for a large breakfast. Thus fuelled, he was ready for anything the day had to offer.

Wednesday morning started identical to the first few days he had been there. As he arrived at the lobby, he spotted a fellow runner he had met on his first run on Monday.

"Good Morning, Heinrich" the man greeted him.

"Good Morning Frank," he replied, "I'll be right with you, I just have to get some water," heading to the hotel newsstand.

"Here," the other man said, offering Heinrich a bottle of the water he normally bought. "I picked up a couple while I was waiting for you."

Heinrich thanked him as he took the bottle and slipped it behind him into the little pocket on his belt. The two men then headed out the door, anxious to get outside to enjoy the morning air.

Their run started with a short jog north along Georgia Street from the downtown core towards Stanley Park. The two men ran easily beside each other, chatting as they went about the previous day's conference. Both in excellent physical condition, they hadn't even broken into a sweat by the time they reached the park. As they approached Lost Lagoon at the entrance to Stanley Park, they moved off the street to the right, following the running path east along Coal Harbour past the Royal Vancouver Yacht Club, towards the Harry Jerome monument and the famous "nine o'clock gun".

"So, Frank," Heinrich said as they ran, "You're saying you didn't listen to any of the papers yesterday?" somewhat puzzled.

"No," Frank replied, "As I told you on Monday, I'm only here to observe . . . you know, how the conference is handled, how the trade show is set up, all those things." He looked across at Heinrich, trying to judge his reaction to his words. "My company is in public relations, trade shows, exhibitions, that sort of thing."

"Of course," replied Heinrich, "I remember now . . . you travel around, trade shows and conferences." Heinrich laughed, shaking his head. "I'm sorry Frank, I talk to fellow scientists all day and overlook the fact that somebody has to actually set these events up."

They continued to run, rounding Brockton Point, pausing only briefly near the little lighthouse to watch a big cruise ship as it left the terminal downtown and headed out into Burrard Inlet. By the time they had run another kilometre along the seawall, they had reached their halfway point for the morning's run.

They paused to take in the stunning view of Vancouver's North Shore mountains, the snow covered "Lions", the famous twin peaks rising above the other mountains. Soon, the huge cruise ship coasted in front of them, turning west towards the Lions Gate Bridge. The morning sun beamed along the inlet, flashing off the wake of the big vessel, lighting up the after decks with a warm glow as the passengers moved around to gain better views of the spectacular scenery that surrounded them. The two men continued their run, feeling they were following the ship as it headed under the bridge on its way to Alaska.

By the time the ship had moved past the bridge and disappeared from view, they had travelled just over another kilometre. At this point, they turned left up a hill into a deeply wooded section of the park, following the road south back towards the entrance to the park, almost two kilometres away. Now sweating slightly, they both sat down on a bench, pulling their water bottles out for a drink. Heinrich always waited until over the halfway mark before he drank, then he drank heartily to keep hydrated. After drinking most of their water, they both felt refreshed and continued up the road.

They had barely started up the hill when Heinrich began to feel winded, his breathing became heavier and more rapid. He fell back a little, moving to the side of the road.

"You O.K. Heinrich?" Frank turned, jogging back to Heinrich, now standing still, gasping for breath.

"I don't know . . . I just can't get my breath" Heinrich wheezed, a look of alarm on his face. "We took this hill on Monday . . . without even raising a sweat."

"Maybe you should just rest a moment," Frank said as he stopped beside him. "Have another drink of water" he said as he reached for Heinrich's water bottle.

Heinrich took it, sipping a little between gasps for air. A tightness in his chest fought against him, preventing his lungs from expanding as they should. A monstrous vice was clamping his chest, tightening up on his heart and lungs. The pains started, hot knives penetrating his heart, making him gasp even more. He staggered, almost falling.

"Jesus, Heinrich, you're getting me worried," Frank said, "You'd better sit down on the side of the road for a few minutes . . . take it easy." As he helped Heinrich sit down, he quickly switched their water bottles and replaced his own in Heinrich's bottle holder. "Better still, why don't you lie down, you might be having a heart attack."

Heinrich's distress increased, a heavy grip on his chest of almost intolerable aching punctuated by stabs of excruciating pain. He lay on the ground, periodically clutching his chest, not knowing what was happening to him, or how to help himself.

"Hey, is everything OK?" they heard from behind them. Another runner had caught up to them, a concerned look on his face.

"I think my friend is having a heart attack, do you have a cell phone?" Frank asked, taking a chance.

"No, I never carry it on these runs, I left it back in the car" the runner said, "maybe we should do CPR on him."

Heinrich appeared to be in more trouble, his breathing becoming shallow and rapid, his eyes pleading for help.

"Good idea," Frank said quickly, "I don't know how, so you go ahead and start, I'll go for help, maybe I can find someone with a phone . . ."

As he started to move away, he looked around to see the man on his knees, starting CPR on Heinrich. He looked at Heinrich, a grim smile creasing his face. "Goodbye, Dr. Kohler" he whispered.

As Heinrich writhed on the ground in pain and confusion, he did not understand what was happening, a stranger now bending over him, pushing on his chest, then lips pressed to his. He vaguely saw his running mate as he turned and faded in the distance.

Frank resumed his run, jogging up the hill and beyond, directly to the park entrance. Continuing up Georgia Street a few blocks, he turned up a side street to a parked car. As he opened the car and climbed in, he scarcely glanced back. His job finished, he drove off, heading south on Georgia Street towards the airport.

CHAPTER 2

L ate that afternoon at the Vancouver Trade and Convention Centre, the conference was almost over when the bad news was made public. Malcolm Thornhill, Chairman of the Global Warming Conference Board interrupted one of the final discussion groups of the closing ceremony to make a special announcement. Plainly upset and troubled by the news, he did not relish the task he had to perform.

"Ladies and Gentlemen . . . excuse me please . . . sorry I interrupted you George . . ." he moved to the podium, stepping up where the moderator had been standing. "Ladies and Gentlemen . . . I'm afraid I have some very bad news . . ." He coughed cleared his throat again as a soft rumble of conversation went around the room. "I'm sorry to end this meeting on such a sad note, but we have just come from a meeting with the Vancouver Police and have confirmed that Dr. Heinrich Kohler, who was scheduled to talk at one of today's sessions, is dead."

Silence hung in the room. Everyone held their breath, waiting, as Malcolm cleared his throat and continued.

"Dr. Kohler was found this morning in Stanley Park, apparently a victim of a fatal heart attack while jogging."

Waves of shock and disbelief rippled through the assembly hall. Everyone turned to express their sorrow or confusion to whoever was sitting beside them.

"As most of you know, Dr. Kohler was a respected member of the scientific community for many years throughout the world, and has been in the forefront of the environmental movement for most of that time. He is probably best known for his dynamic theories and controversial views and opinions, culminating in his presentation about eight years ago of his now famous "Kohler Effect", describing the distinct possibility of an irreversible chain reaction in the global warming phenomenon. Because of this work, we have been warned of one of the most dangerous threats to mankind today." Malcolm paused, his voice breaking slightly.

The audience took the pause as an invitation for questions.

"Mr. Thornhill, Stanley Park is a busy place this time of year . . . why has it taken all day for this news to reach us?"

"From what the police say, he was found early this morning by another jogger, probably very soon after he collapsed. He was taken immediately to St. Paul's Hospital, but was pronounced dead on arrival. Unfortunately, they didn't know who he was. He had no identification, only his jogging clothes and a bottle of water. He did have his hotel key, so the police managed to trace him that way. Once in his room, they found who he was through his passport and other papers, and that he was a delegate in this conference. It was later this afternoon before they contacted us for further confirmation and identification."

A local reporter asked the next question, sending shockwaves through the group.

"Not every one bought into his theories," she began, "I recall when he first announced them that many politicians and scientists around the world thought they were 'over exaggerations' and 'alarmist ideas'. Have the police ruled out foul play?"

Taken aback by the question, Malcolm was momentarily at a loss for words.

"I . . . I can only repeat what we have been told by the police . . . he was out running, and had a heart attack." He paused again, picking up his single sheet of notes as if to leave. Another question from the floor stopped him.

"Mr. Malcolm . . . Dr. Kohler was scheduled to present another paper this morning."

"That's correct." Malcolm answered, knowing what was coming.

"The title and abstract are listed in the schedule, but the paper is not included in the publications we received. Can you explain this . . . and will we be receiving a copy?"

"Yes and No." Malcolm replied, disturbed by the question and even more disturbed by the answer he had to give. "After Dr. Kohler's paper was received for review and acceptance, and eventually placed on our agenda, Dr. Kohler recalled all copies, saying he had to make some revisions and corrections, and that he would be bringing all of the final copies for distribution during the conference."

"Isn't that rather unusual?"

"Yes, and in most cases not even allowed. In this case, based on Dr. Kohler's reputation and the importance of the paper, normal rules were waived and we accepted Dr. Kohler's promise. Unfortunately, we shall never hear that paper."

More waves of confused comments and questions rumbled through the room. Malcolm tapped the podium one more time.

"I'm sorry, I can't answer any more questions at this time. The Board will be issuing a written press release later today with any updates on the information as we receive them. I'm sure those of you who knew Heinrich will join me in an expression of sadness and deepest sympathy for his family."

Jake Prescott sat in the rear of the hall, his mouth gaping in disbelief. Sadness welled up within him, replacing the utter shock of hearing that one of his best friends had just died. Stunned, his gaze was fixed on the podium in front of the room, his eyes filling with tears.

"Jake . . . you O.K.?" his friend asked. Alan Cook was more than a friend, he was Jake's lab manager and chief chemist at Prescott Industries. The two had decided to visit the conference together as most of the significant papers they were interested in were covered during this last day of the conference.

"Yeah, I'm fine," Jake replied, shaking his head, "I still don't believe it . . . I was just talking to Heinrich yesterday . . . we had lunch and a few beers on the weekend after he arrived, so I was surprised this afternoon when he didn't show up to present his paper. I . . ." he faltered.

"Jake relax," Alan said quietly, "Come on, let's go have a drink somewhere." He grabbed Jake by the arm and led him out of the room, heading down the long hallway towards one of the many bars and dining lounges in the centre. Before long, they were comfortably seated in a dark corner with a couple of drinks in front of them.

Alan was the first to speak, holding up his glass in a toast.

"Cheers! Here's to Heinrich . . . I never knew him, but if he was a friend of yours Jake, he must have been one damn fine bloke."

Jake laughed, seeing the humour in Alan's typical Aussie assessment of Heinrich as "one damn fine bloke".

"Yes Alan, he was that!" He laughed again, knowing that Heinrich, a scientist and university professor would also see the humour of being called "One damn fine bloke". He raised his glass and they both drank heartily to Heinrich.

"I was just thinking," Jake began, "I've known Heinrich for over fifteen years. We first met in Munich, at the university . . . Ludwig-Maximilians . . . back when I was recovering at Stefan's place after my folks were killed." Alan listened carefully, knowing Jake normally did not talk much about some of his troubled past. Jake continued.

"It was just after I finished here at U.B.C., I was visiting my parents in Germany. As you know, we were all involved in a horrendous car accident - they were killed and I barely survived left with this bad leg," gesturing with his cane. "I stayed with our old friends to recover, Stefan Schiller and his young daughter, Christa. It was good therapy, I brushed up on my German, learned a lot about Bavaria, Austria and Switzerland, and eventually went back to university in Munich to pick up another degree." He paused for another sip of his drink. "Call that waiter over again Alan, let's get some peanuts or nachos or something . . . I think we'll be here for awhile." Alan waved his hand to attract the waiter's attention.

"Heinrich was teaching at the university then. He's from Austria, actually . . . just outside of Bregenz." Alan's face had a question mark written all over it. "In case you're wondering, Bregenz is a small town at the southeast end of the Bodensee . . . what you call Lake Constance." Alan's head nodded, now that he knew where Jake was talking about. "Heinrich had spent some time in the environmental monitoring centre in Bregenz, but too many universities wanted him to join them, offers of research money, teaching jobs, the whole thing! So he did the best of both worlds . . . all of the above! When I met him . . . he was one of my professors . . . we clashed several times, but always he would listen to my ideas, pushed me the way nobody had ever pushed me. By the end of that year, we were great friends and I used to visit him in Bregenz on holidays, we used to go hiking together in the *Bregenzerwald,* or up in the forested hills above Bregenz." Jake paused again, a troubled look on his face. "That's the weird thing about this . . . Heinrich was always in good shape, he could out-hike me any day . . . and he used to run everywhere! For him to drop dead of a heart attack is hard to accept."

"It happens Jake," Alan offered, "Just look at all the first class athletes that have dropped in their prime. How old was Heinrich . . . forty, fifty?"

"Probably more like fifty at least." Jake answered, finally accepting the possibility.

"Is he married?" Alan asked.

"He was when I knew him years ago . . . but his wife was killed in a car accident about eight years ago . . . about the same time as when he released the 'Kohler Affect' paper. That really hit him hard . . . I thought for sure he would give up." Jake stopped, many memories flooding back. "He's lived with his sister Helga ever since. She's an older woman, never married. She's going to take this hard . . . Jesus, I always seem to be going to Europe to a funeral!"

Alan absorbed the comments and the history, filling in some of the gaps in his own knowledge of Jake Prescott. Jake was a self made millionaire and still under forty. Alan had learned much of Jake's more recent background from an incident that had happened less than a year before, so he was glad to learn more about his early days. Apparently after picking up another degree in Germany, Jake had spent a few years in the foreign service, specializing in communications and computer technology, travelling in Europe, South America and Japan. His language skills were legendary, as well as his expertise in martial arts. He married, only to lose his wife after two years to cancer. Devastated, he quit the service and returned home to start his own business. After several years of hard work and poverty, he finally hit it big, devising a new technique for analysis that put the business into the big time. After a couple of years of stress, strain, and considerable success, Jake sold out to a large corporation, making enough to be comfortable for the rest of his life. Since then he had kept a small core of friends and experts to handle occasional consulting and specialized studies.

The previous summer, after a deadly environmental terrorism scare in Los Angeles, Jake found himself and the entire crew involved in an international chase to find the answers and the people behind them. A bloody climax in Germany resulted in a special laboratory being blown up with his old friend and mentor Stefan Schiller killed along with his beautiful daughter, Christa.

Although several of the 'terrorists' were killed in the fracas, the leader of the group escaped, the one that had killed Jake's friend and lover. Jake's love for Christa was rarely discussed, but was well known in the company, another tragic chapter in the troubled life of Jake Prescott.

CHAPTER 3

The following morning found Jake in his office, trying to catch up on a little paperwork. He couldn't get Heinrich's death out of his mind, and he was about to call Malcolm Thornhill for more details when his intercom buzzed.

"Yes, Shannon?"

"Mr. Prescott, there are two detectives here from the Vancouver Police . . . do you have a minute to talk to them?"

Jake paused before answering. Shannon never called him "Mr. Prescott" unless it was serious business. This was her way of warning him about something, but because it was the police, he really didn't need the warning.

"O.K. Shannon, please bring them in," he replied.

Shannon entered the room with two plainclothes officers and made introductions before leaving.

"Please sit gentlemen, what can I do for you?"

"Mr. Prescott . . ."

"Please, call me Jake," Jake interrupted. "I feel a lot more comfortable."

"O.K. Jake," Pete Johnson, the first officer replied. "This is in regards to a Dr. Heinrich Kohler, who you know was found dead yesterday." Before Jake had a chance to respond, the detective continued. "The hotel records show that you made two telephone calls to his room from your cell phone, and also left a message with the hotel telephone operator."

"Yes . . ."

"Can you tell us what the calls were for, and what connection you had with Dr. Kohler?"

At first, Jake started to feel angry, then realized they had to check everything out, make sure there was no "foul play", as the reporter asked yesterday.

"Dr. Kohler is . . . was . . . an old friend," Jake started, "In fact, he was my professor in university years ago, and I've been a friend of the family for years. As for the calls, Heinrich was scheduled to present a paper . . . make a speech yesterday at the conference. When he didn't show up, I'm sure there were a lot of calls made, we were all trying to find him." The second detective, Neil Hagen, was taking notes as Jake talked. Jake continued "Where is Heinrich now . . . where are his personal effects . . . has his sister been informed . . . when will the body be released?"

"Whoa . . . wait a minute Jake," Johnson interrupted him, "We're supposed to ask the questions. Why are you so interested?"

"He was my friend, for Christ sake!" Jake blurted out. "Also, I know his sister, and I'll have to fly to Europe for the funeral, so I'd like to know what the situation is before I talk to her."

"Of course, I'm sorry," Johnson replied. "Dr. Kohler's body is presently at the coroner's office, waiting for an autopsy. It would have been done yesterday, but we've been backlogged."

"Autopsy?" Jake asked. "I thought . . . we were told it was a heart attack."

"That was only a first guess, an initial diagnosis when he was first brought in, but in these situations, the coroner likes to confirm what he died from, especially when there are complications."

"Complications? What kind of complications?" Jake asked, still in shock.

"We'll get into that later. In the meantime, all his stuff is at our office until we finish our investigation," Hagen replied,

"Normally, it would all be sent to next of kin, but if you are going . . ."

"Yes," said Jake. "please let me know."

The two detectives glanced at each other, a silent communication. Pete Johnson turned to Jake with another question.

"Jake, did you know any of Dr. Kohler's friends or associates?"

"Some, yes, but . . ."

"Specifically, do you know if he was jogging with anyone while he was here?"

"No, I don't know . . . he really didn't know anyone here except myself, and possibly a few casual acquaintances in the scientific community, maybe someone here for the conference. He arrived last Saturday . . . I picked him up at his hotel on Sunday and we went out for some lunch and a few drinks."

"Jake, would you mind coming down to our Cambie Street office to look at something for us?"

"Yes, of course, but what . . .?"

"We have some of Dr. Kohler's personal things there, as well as a security tape we would like you to see."

"When would . . ."

"As soon as you could find the time . . . now if possible."

The mystery was too much for Jake and he agreed to go immediately. Heinrich was his friend and he would do whatever necessary to clear up any confusion about his death. As he left his office, he told Shannon what was happening and said he would be back soon. The detectives agreed to drive him so they could talk on the way.

"Actually, Jake," Johnson started as they headed towards downtown Vancouver. "We haven't been totally honest with you."

Jake's defences went up immediately. "Oh?" he asked, "In what way?"

"Two things, first, we know more about you than we let on . . . for instance, we know you worked with Interpol and the FBI last year on that terrorism thing in Germany, so we had an idea your acquaintance with Kohler was legitimate."

Jake was surprised at how fast they had collected that information, then thought they probably have all this on file downtown all the time.

"And the second thing you haven't told me?" Jake asked, not offering anything.

"Well, you might find this interesting," Johnson started, "There were actually two people found dead in the park. Your friend Kohler, and another man, a John McGee. Do you know him?"

Jake couldn't believe what he was hearing. "What, when did you know this, how come we haven't heard anything about a second man?" he yelled at the officers.

"Need to know Jake. We did not want to let that information out right away, in case it affected our investigation. That is one of the 'complications' I referred to earlier. He was found laying across Dr. Kohler, looks like he was trying CPR on him or something. As I asked before, do you know him?"

"No, I don't know him, who is he?" asked Jake. "Was he part of the conference?"

"No, it appears the poor bugger was just another runner who happened to come along at the wrong time."

"Are you saying this guy just happened to come along, tried a little CPR on Heinrich, then dropped dead almost immediately? What ever it was, it sure acts fast!" Jake felt they were missing something important.

"One thing we do know, he was not Kohler's usual running partner. From our talks with the hotel staff, specifically front desk . . . Kohler went jogging on Monday, Tuesday and Wednesday mornings . . . each day with the same man, a guy he met each morning in the lobby. We have confirmed it was not this McGee guy. Only on Wednesday, neither of them returned."

"Who was this other man?" asked Jake, suddenly interested.

"That's the question we've been asking," Hagen said as he dodged traffic coming off the Oak Street bridge. "From what the hotel people say, he wasn't staying there. We can only guess he was at another hotel and went to Kohler's hotel each morning to meet him."

"Do you have a description of the man . . . ?"

"We have more than that . . . we have a video tape of him."

"A video . . . what . . .?"

"The hotel has security cameras covering the lobby and a few other key areas. Luckily, we have tapes of Kohler and his running partner on Wednesday . . . they're still trying to find if they have one for the other days."

"So that's the tapes you wanted me to look at." asked Jake.

"Yes . . . on the odd chance you might recognize him, or know something about him."

"I guess it's worth a try." Jake commented, not really believing it would do much good.

Before long, they were heading down Cambie Street towards the city and within minutes were pulling into the parking lot of the Cambie Street Police Station. As they left the car and headed into the building, Jake felt the excitement rising within himself, an excitement he had not felt for almost a year. Quick flashes of memories went through his mind, scenes of violence and death as they fought for their life in a hunting lodge in the Bavarian Alps. A battle that saw his lover Christa shot down together with her father, Jake's long time friend and mentor. The sadness of the memories overcame the brief feeling of excitement as he limped into the building.

"Jake . . . Jake, you O.K.?" Hagen was shaking his arm.

Pulled back to the present, Jake replied "Yeah, I'm O.K., just thinking about something, sorry."

The two detectives escorted him into a small room equipped with a television set and a VCR player. Hagen had already retrieved the tape and set it up to play.

"Just before we play the tape, take a look at this." he said, turning to Heinrich's personal effects. "Just in case anything might ring a bell, you know, you might spot something."

Jake looked, expecting the experience to be painful. A suitcase, a small briefcase containing a laptop computer, a small collection of literature and technical papers from the conference, several plastic ziplock bags of personal things, shaver, toothbrush, shampoo. Jake shook his head, then scanned the collection again, his eyes resting on the technical papers.

"Tell me," he asked, "Were there more copies of papers like this in his brief case or suitcase?"

"No," Hagen replied, scanning an inventory list he held. "Just those ones . . . apparently they were given out at the conference to all delegates."

"Yes, I know," said Jake, "All except Heinrich's paper . . . I thought a copy of his paper might be here." He looked around again. "How about the computer, have you checked it?"

"No, not yet. If you'd like, we'll check that before you go back to your office . . . you'll probably have a better idea of what to look for than we would."

Jake agreed as they sat down to watch the video tape. Hagen handled the remote control. "I'll play a little standard stuff before I jump ahead to the good part" he said, as if he were showing a good movie.

Jake watched, a night scene of the hotel lobby in living black and white, as a few people came and went in jerky movements of about one frame per second.

"The tape is changed every day at midnight, so this is very early morning . . . not a hell of a lot of activity." Hagen added. As soon as they were familiar with the background, Hagen fast-forwarded the tape to almost seven AM. A few more people were moving around, entering and leaving the elevator and the front door. A man stood off to one side as Heinrich walked off the elevator into the lobby. Jake's eyes were fixed on Heinrich, looking the same as when they had gone for lunch on the weekend. He watched as Heinrich talked to the other man, took a bottle of water from him and headed out the door.

"See anything, Jake?" asked Johnson. "Do you know this man, or have you seen him before?"

Jake realized he had been so fixed on Heinrich that he hadn't even looked at the other man. "I'm sorry, could you play it again?" he asked, a little embarrassed.

"No problem." Hagen said as he backed it up and started again.

Heinrich walked out of the elevator towards the other man . . . the other man . . . Jake jumped up, eyes fixed on the screen. He stopped breathing, his heart thumped wildly as he stared at the face, visible for only a second.

"Back, back . . . again," he whispered, not taking his eyes off the scene in front of him. Hagen played it again.

Jake stared as the tape played through.

"Stop!" he screamed as the man became visible.

Hagen froze the tape, then started zooming in to the face of the man until the quality of the image started to break up. He turned to Jake, realizing he had recognized the man. "Do you know this man?" he asked Jake.

Jake could hardly breath, his entire body trembling with hate. He gasped a breath, then quietly whispered "The devil himself! Landau . . . Kurt Landau!"

CHAPTER 4

Jake stood still, eyes locked on the grainy image of the face on the television screen. It was unmistakably Landau, the rounded face with dark eyebrows over deep-set black eyes. His hair was a little thinner, but still combed back, accentuating his broad forehead even more. Jake's mind was also replaying a scene from the past, the same face obscured by smoke and steam, a gun pointed at him, more puffs of smoke as the barrel of the gun kicked up, the sickening impact and slow relaxation as his Christa expired in his arms.

"Jake . . . Jake . . ." Neil Hagen's words sounded vaguely in Jake's ears. "How do you know this man?" he continued, knowing the connection was strong.

Jake finally controlled himself, the shock and hatred slowing growing into a sense of excitement, a sense of purpose, a real feeling that after all, he might have his revenge on the monster that killed his lover and friend.

He slowly turned to the two detectives, shaking his head slightly. "I can't believe that son-of-a-bitch was right here in Vancouver!" Walking over to the collection of Heinrich's personal effects, he looked down at the pitiful pile that represented his good friend.

Both detectives watched, waited, expecting Jake to respond. The glazed look in Jake's eyes slowly cleared and he became aware of the two men. He turned to them, answering Hagen's question.

"You want information on this guy? . . . check with Interpol . . . call Jacques Manet in Lyon, a British agent who worked with me in Germany last year." Jake waved back Hagen who obviously had a another question. "I know, a name like Jacques Manet doesn't sound British, but it's a long story . . . if you talk to Jacques, I'm sure he can fill you in. In any case, Kurt Landau was responsible for almost all of the deaths in that shoot-out in Bavaria. He disappeared shortly after and I think they've been looking for him ever since!"

"Jesus Christ!" Johnson breathed, "This is really getting to be more than just a poor jogger folding up in the park!"

"But why?" Jake asked. "Why does a scum-bag like Landau come to Vancouver to kill Heinrich Kohler, what's the point?"

"I don't know Jake," answered detective Hagen, "But we're going to find out. First, let's take another look at that tape, back a few minutes, before Kohler shows up."

He backed up the tape to almost six o'clock, then started it again at normal speed. There was less activity, fewer people moving around, a couple with suitcases leaving for an early flight. Landau showed up about six-thirty, taking a seat in the lobby.

"What's he got in his hands?" Jake asked.

Neil played the tape slower, "Looks like a couple of bottles of water."

Nothing much happened until about seven, when Landau stood up and started pacing the lobby, obviously waiting for Heinrich.

"O.K., here comes Kohler . . . watch what happens." Pete said. As they watched, the two men met, obviously greeting each other. Heinrich turned towards the newsstand, then turned back, taking one of the bottles from Landau's hand and placing it in his belt.

"Damn!" yelled Pete, "the water . . . that's how he did it!"

"Are you saying he put something in Heinrich's water?" Jake asked.

"I'm just saying it's a possibility." Pete answered.

"Was there any left when he was taken to the hospital? Can you test the water?"

"This Landau looks like a pretty smooth character," Neil said, "he probably changed the bottles back after it had done the job. I'll alert the coroner's office about this possibility, they can run a toxicology test on both the water bottle and his stomach contents."

He turned and picked up a phone and made two quick calls. He then turned to his partner. "O.K. Pete, the coroner will make sure some extra TOX screens are run, our computer people will make some blow-up copies of Landau's face from this tape . . . then we'll get on the blower to this Manet guy in Interpol, maybe get a better photo and some more information."

Jake looked at his watch. "It's almost nine in the evening there, so Jacques is probably at home. In any case, his office can get the information you require." Something continued to nag at Jake's thoughts. "On those tests Neil, the ones on his stomach contents, you probably won't find anything. Heinrich would've noticed if the bottle had been opened, you know, those bottles all have the plastic caps sealed. Besides, this is not a normal poison, it acted too fast . . . not only on Heinrich, but also on that second guy. I'll ask my chemist back at the office, he's good at these things."

Pete Johnson was deep in thought, still trying to get a handle on all of the facts. "Tell me Jake, you've been involved with both of these people much longer than we have. Can you think of anything . . . anything at all that might have triggered this? First . . . do you think they knew each other before Vancouver?"

Jake thought about it, not wanting to admit that Heinrich could have known Landau. "I really don't know for sure . . . I suppose there is a possibility. Heinrich has been doing research and still teaches at the university in Munich. He also still hangs out with some of his old crew from the environmental centre in

Bregenz. He speaks and teaches at least a half-dozen universities across Europe on an invitational basis when he's not up north."

"Up north?"

"Yes, part of an ongoing research project he's been involved with in the Arctic."

"Christ, that's a lot of ground to cover!" Pete answered.

Jake continued. "As far as Landau is concerned, he's got training in the N.S.O., both in the U.S. and East Germany. It was most likely in East Germany that he learned all his dirty tricks. He was *Spetsnaz,* and learned special skills and made a lot of useful contacts he could use later. He speaks a half-dozen languages, English, Russian and German among his fluent ones. Apparently, when he worked for Steinbock as head of security, he hired a lot of his buddies and even some of his old *Spetsnaz* enemies to work with him, eventually taking over the entire security division. What he's been up to since then . . . I have no idea. He could have connections anywhere, I just don't know."

"Whoa, wait a second Jake." asked Pete. "What is this Spetsnaz, for us uninformed with international spook stuff?"

Jake laughed, realizing these men only dealt with local crimes, with very little need or necessity for involving foreign organizations. "*Spetsnaz* comes from the two Russian words 'spetsialnogo naznacheniya', which basically mean 'special forces'. In English, we use the term when referring to Russian Special Forces specifically. These are real mean dudes, elite special forces in certain crack units in the Russian military. Actually, there were different divisions, some operated by the KGB or the GRU, all used for special purposes."

The two detectives hung on his every word, mouths slack, a fascinating diversion from their everyday detective work.

"Well, maybe Interpol will tell us something." Neil finally offered. He turned to leave the room. "I'll go and make some calls, you guys check out the computer."

Jake stopped him before he left. "If you want information right away, try the Interpol's N.C.B. in Washington... that's their North American office, or try Bert Jackson at the F.B.I. there . . . he is definitely familiar with Mr. Landau. Once you get the ball rolling, you can call Manet early tomorrow morning for the real up-to-date stuff."

"O.K., thanks Jake." Before he left, he turned back to Jake and asked "Jake . . . just out of curiosity . . . you seem to know this Manet fellow pretty good. From what you say, you worked with him on that Germany thing."

"Yes, right up to the final shoot-out!" Jake replied.

"But how come Manet was involved, how come he was in the field . . . Interpol officers don't normally operate like that, certainly don't have running gun-battles with the bad guys. Contrary to popular belief, there aren't any Interpol "agents", they leave the police work up to the local police."

"Yes, I know," Jake replied, "I've been through this a dozen times. Jacques came to Frankfurt to warn me about some mercenaries, and to find out some more information that only I had at the time. Unfortunately, we had already left on a river barge and were attacked by the mercenaries that night. The entire case started to become personal for Jacques, everywhere he turned, he was blocked, frustrated. It took two days for Jacques to finally find me in a hospital in Germany . . . and things deteriorated from there. He wasn't really acting as a field agent, I was. It seemed that everywhere we went, everywhere I suggested we go, something happened. We always tried the get the local police involved, but by the time they arrived, it was all over!"

They both looked at Jake, shaking their heads. "I think I'm going to enjoy working with you Jake," Pete said, "But you're like a loose cannon, you never know what's going to happen next!"

Jake laughed "That's exactly what Jacques told me when we first met!"

Neil finally left the office and Pete turned to Heinrich's belongings, moving them all to one of the table.

"O.K., let's start from the beginning again . . . now that we know someone else is definitely involved here, maybe we'll see things differently." He began by picking up each item, inspecting it closely, and asked Jake to also look at it to make sure it did not trigger any memories, suspicions, or additional information.

"Did you find an address book or an electronic organizer of some kind?" Jake asked.

"No, nothing so obvious. We thought maybe he might have something in his computer . . . we'll check that in a minute."

They continued with each item, each piece of paper, nothing seemed out of place or unusual.

"Here's his plane ticket," Pete explained, flipping the pages of the electronic printout. "He flew from Zürich on Friday, changing planes in Toronto, then on directly to Vancouver. He must have driven to the Zürich airport." He continued to look through some papers in Heinrich's wallet. "Tell me Jake, he has two addresses listed here . . . one in Bregenz, Austria, and one in Munich, Germany."

"His official address is his sister's place in Bregenz. He also has an apartment in Munich, near the university."

"Of course."

Jake continued as something occurred to him. "You just suggested he must have driven to Zürich . . . did you find a car park ticket, or even car keys?"

"Not yet, but that doesn't mean anything. When you park in those places for a few days or a week, they usually keep your keys . . . pull out your car when you return." He kept looking. "But I agree, he should have a claim ticket of some kind here."

They finally finished checking every single item, eventually finding the parking claim ticket in his jacket pocket.

"Just when I thought things were getting interesting." Jake commented. "Do you want to check the computer now?"

Glancing at his watch, Pete motioned to Jake to follow him. "After lunch . . . come on, we can grab a burger up the street. I'll get Neil to join us."

The weather was warm and sunny as the three men walked a few blocks up Cambie street to a Wendy's restaurant. After fighting their way through a crowd of teens, they settled into a corner table overlooking the street.

Neil was the first to talk. "O.K., I've talked to the Washington office of Interpol . . . they're going to fax some information to us this afternoon. I haven't talked to the F.B.I. guy yet, but I've left a message for him to call me."

"Can you tell me Jake," started Pete, "what was so important about this Dr. Kohler, and what is so important about this technical paper he was supposed to have?"

Jake munched on his burger, collecting his thoughts. A few more fries and a quick sip from his drink and he looked across to the two men.

"I'm sure you've both heard about global warming, greenhouse gases, all that kind of thing?" Both men were nodding their heads, mouths full of lunch. "I mean, who hasn't heard about it? Well, about ten or twelve years ago, Heinrich was lecturing some of his ideas and theories about these problems. Nobody took him seriously, in fact, many were upset by the idea that man's pollution was the source of our problems. Then about eight years ago, he presented a technical paper on the subject, along with some interesting proof and a new theory about a possible irreversible effect . . . kind of a point of no return theory . . . a chain reaction in global warming that would eventually wipe us all out! That is an over-simplification of the idea, but it became known as the "Kohler effect". It hit the media for a few months, but like many important issues, it became yesterday's news, and was forgotten. A few countries are trying to change things, but very little has actually been accomplished globally. The powers that be keep meeting, holding conferences in Rio, Montreal, Kyoto, Nairobi, spending millions of entertainment dollars, then making promises they know they either will not, or cannot keep. This is the stuff that Al Gore has been running around the world with for years, talking and trying to get some politicians to listen to him. The announcements a while back from the conference in Beijing indicate things are a lot worse than they thought. Again, this stuff will float around in the press for a short time, then disappear."

"So is that where Kohler's new paper comes in?" Pete asked.

"We don't know for sure . . . Heinrich told me a few things on Sunday, but even I haven't seen the paper. From what he told me, yes, it's more of the same, only worse! He has integrated some of the results of his Arctic research, and it comes down to this . . . we either change our ways . . . big time, or we could see the end of mankind as we know it within couple of generations!"

"The end of mankind!" Pete coughed, almost choking on a mouth full of fries. "Jesus Christ!" he grinned widely, "I guess that's why I love this job!"

CHAPTER 5

Jake's phone rang, interrupting their lunch. He answered it, talking briefly to his secretary, Shannon. Turning to the others, he put his hand over the phone.

"It's Helga, Heinrich's sister, calling from Austria . . . Shannon's connecting her through now."

Jake listened again. There were a couple of clicks on the line and the sobbing voice of Heinrich's sister filled Jake's little phone.

"*Grüss Gott, Helga, wie geht's . . . Was machs du?*" His face took on a grim appearance as he listened. The two detectives glanced at each other, realizing this was an important call, but unable to participate or understand even one end of the conversation. After several minutes of talking, Jake finally closed up his phone, turning his attention to the two men.

"As I said before, that was Helga Kohler. Sounds like she's been a basket case ever since she was notified about Heinrich."

"How's she doin' now . . . why did she call?" Neil asked.

Jake didn't reply right away, but was trying to make sense of Helga's call. "She just got home, she was at a friend's place overnight. Her place has been broken into . . . just Heinrich's room . . . everything's upside down, she has no idea what was taken."

"Why did she call you, has she called the police?"

"Yes, she did that first, but she knows I talked to Heinrich since he arrived, and I'll be curious about his death. I guess I'm her last resort, and she's hoping I can make some sense of all this."

"I'd like to make a little sense of it myself," Pete answered, slurping the last of his large root beer. "Tell me again about this paper Kohler was supposed to have. Is this thing that important . . . worth a burglary to find it, or worse, worth killing for?"

"That's what makes this whole thing crazy," Jake answered. "It's just a technical paper! Most of these papers are just the results of a study or some experiments, sometimes a different method of operation or manufacturing. They are not usually anything revolutionary . . . no "secret formulas", or anything worth killing someone for."

"Well Jake," Pete replied as he put on his jacket. "Somebody thinks there is . . . and that's what we have to find out. Come on, let's get back and check out that computer."

As they headed back to the station, Jake asked "I have my own theories on this," he said slowly, "but are you saying now that Heinrich was murdered?"

Pete answered quickly. "Officially, we won't know until we have the coroner's report, the tox results, everything, but I'm willing to bet right now that your man Landau gave Kohler something in his drink . . . something that didn't agree with him!"

"Besides the drink, check around his lips, mouth, see if there is any residue," Jake offered, "Think about it guys, it would have to be something that wasn't washed away by the water, something that the second guy would be exposed to." He then added "and send some of the sample to our lab like the first ones."

He pulled out his cell-phone again and dialed his office. "Hi Shannon, could I speak with Alan?" He turned to the detectives to explain. "Alan Cook is my lab manager, an Aussie who got lost on a trip to Canada, one of the best chemists in the business. He specializes in environmental things, but I can usually count on him for weird things like this." He paused a moment, then said,

"Alan, I've got a little puzzle for you." Jake continued to describe what little information he had been told about Heinrich's death so far, together with the death of the second person. "Basically Alan, I think the rapid death of the second man is an important clue. We want to know what kind of poison causes a heart attack, or seizures, within minutes of taking or touching it? We'll be back in the office is a little while, see what you can come up with. I've asked the police to have a duplicate sample sent to you, please run them as soon as possible, these guys are backed up with their system."

"Christ, nothing like a challenge!" muttered Neil.

They were soon back at the station. Both detectives stopped to pick up messages before they walked down the hall to the room where they had watched the tape. Jake said nothing as he walked across the room and set up Heinrich's laptop computer on the table. Turning it on, they all waited as the system booted up. Within seconds the screen lit up with a Windows logo while small beeps and other sounds emanated from the little speakers. They waited patiently, eyes glued to the screen.

"Do you know what to look for?" Neil asked.

"Not really," Jake answered. "We'll just look for word processing files, a report of some kind. Depending on how much stuff he keeps on this hard drive, it could take some time to check out all the files," said Jake, facing the detective.

"Is it supposed to look like that?" Neil asked, pointing to the screen.

Jake turned, looking at the screen a little closer. The Windows logo and all the text on the screen were sagging downward, like they had turned to a liquid and were starting to flow off the screen. At first, Jake thought it was one of the new screen-saver programs, where everything moves around or falls apart. This one is a little different, he thought as he hit one of the keys, usually the trigger to stop a screen-saver. He reached for the little mouse pad in the centre of the keyboard, but whatever he did, it just seemed to accelerate the process.

"Damn!" yelled Jake, hands flying over the keyboard. "I hope this isn't what I think it is!"

"What is it?" Pete asked. "We got a problem?"

"We have a virus . . . a very clever virus that was triggered as soon as we booted the system." They watched helplessly as the screen appeared to slowly melt down into a pool, a nondescript collection of various colours and pieces of text from above.

Everything jumped violently as Jake's fist hit the table.

"What the hell's going on?" Pete's confusion was apparent. "I'm no computer geek, so you'll have to explain all this."

His partner stepped in and tried to describe what had just happened. "I'm no expert either, but I think we've just been screwed! Someone has planted a virus in Kohler's system, a self-destructing one."

Jake nodded, his attempts to stop the process futile. He finally gave up, turning the computer off.

"You're right Neil, it has probably wiped everything on the hard drive. It'll have to be completely cleaned and reformatted. In any case, it's no use to us." He checked the laptop one more time, ejecting a disk out of the CD drive. "Were there any more disks in his brief case?" he asked as he looked at the writing on the disk. "This is just some free demo disk," he said as he tossed it into the case.

Neil handed him three additional CD's. "This is all we could find," he said.

"Do you guys have some good anti-virus protection on your computers?" Jake asked. "If not, I'll take these back to my office and turn them over to my computer expert. I'll have him check for viruses, then tell us what's on them."

CHAPTER 6

It didn't take Peter Wong very long to confirm what Jake had suggested earlier at the police station. The virus was quite new and very deadly. Peter had already heard about it on one of the internet virus info-centres, so was prepared with the latest protection from his internet security provider. He called Jake into the lab after about an hour. The two detectives had driven Jake back to the office and had decided to stay for the demonstration.

"Watch this Jake," he said, as he inserted a disk into a computer on the bench. "That's the demo disk you found . . . has a neat personal organizer program, something that would appeal to everyone, especially a scientist like Kohler."

"What computer are you using?" asked Jake, a concerned look on his face.

"Don't worry, this is one of those old units we were going to scrap. Even if it wasn't, we could always fix it up after . . . anyway, watch. First, I insert the disk. Now at this point I could either just run a directory to see what is on it, or I could follow the "run demo" instructions that are on the disk, which I will do now."

The computer read the disk, bringing up a nice little personal organizer utility program. Peter ran it through a few of the features, printed something, then shut down the program. He then ran a word processor program off the computer hard disk, typed a few words, then closed it as well.

"See . . . so far, so good. This is really clever, because up to now, you don't even realize you've been screwed. You can even remove the disk." He removed the disk and shut down the computer. "Nothing happens until you restart the computer . . . like you guys did at the police station. Watch."

Once again, Jake waited as the computer started up, displaying all the graphics and sounds they normally have, then watched with fascination as the same fluidization of the screen occurred, dripping everything to the bottom of the screen.

"Jeez, that's the same thing that happened back at the station!" Neil said, fascinated by the demonstration.

"You were right, it also wipes the hard drive," Peter added, "This is the second one I've tried. Whatever Dr. Kohler had on that drive is gone . . . someone made sure of that."

"O.K., we've lost that. What was on the other disks we found in the case?" Jake asked.

"Nothing . . . at least nothing worth mentioning. One was blank, one had some spreadsheets for some air quality data, and the other had some lecture material in German for a university in Munich."

"That's interesting, Peter," Jake said, "you don't speak German, how did you know it was lecture material?"

"Each lecture had two files, one in English, one in German . . . that much I could figure out."

"Peter, do you know for sure the virus came from this disk, the little demo utility program?" asked Jake.

"Yeah, it's there alright! I haven't had a chance to look at it closely yet, but maybe later we can get an idea about where it came from, maybe even who wrote the code."

Jake turned to his two shadows for the day. "O.K., what do we have? Heinrich might or might not have had his paper on his laptop. In any case, someone gave him a demo to try . . . it could have been anyone at the conference, or our friend Mr. Landau.

They might have talked about computers and Landau might have given the disk to Heinrich to try."

"O.K. Jake," answered Pete Johnson, "But we keep coming back to the same question . . . why?"

"That's what we have to find out," Jake answered, turning to his intercom. "Alan, if you're ready, could you come in please?"

Alan Cook entered the office, loaded with papers and reference books which he spread out before them.

"Any luck?" Jake asked after he had introduced Alan to the two detectives.

"OK mates, I hope you find this as interesting as I have!" He turned to Jake and added "Bloody hell, Jake, you really come up with some corkers. I went through my entire list of poisons and toxic substances. Hardly anything reacts the way you described. Then I started getting into some real exotic things. My first guess was tetrodotoxin, the stuff from pufferfish - fugu, you most likely ran into that in Japan, Jake," he asked.

"I've heard of it, but I've never tried it" remembering that literally hundreds of people have been killed from improperly prepared fugu in restaurants in Japan and there were still hundreds more poisoned each year.

"Well, no matter, I've eliminated that because it acts too slow for your case. It usually takes from twenty minutes to three hours for the symptoms to appear from fugu poisoning."

"So what's your next choice?" Jake asked, knowing Alan would have something up his sleeve.

"How about Batrachotoxin?"

This was met with blank stares by the others. "What the hell is that?" asked Pete.

"Batrachotoxin is an extremely potent cardiotoxic and neurotoxic steroidal alkaloid." He paused for effect, raising two fingers emphatically. "Remember those two words gentlemen, 'cardiotoxic and neurotoxic', our two big problems. Batrachotoxin is the most potent of the toxins in the dendrobatidae family - it's a tropical thing . . . secreted on the skin of certain types of Phyllobates species frogs - commonly called 'poison dart' frogs." Alan was getting wound up, enjoying his moment of glory. "Local natives in the jungle or wherever put this stuff on their arrows, actually little darts that they shoot at birds or small animals, kills them within seconds." Alan looked at them all, his face grim as he shook his head.

"Is this the same as curare?" asked one of the detectives. "I heard they use that in South America somewhere on blow-gun darts".

"Hell, this is even worse than curare, like about fifteen times more deadly! "Blimey, Jake, this stuff is bad, like real bad! It is about ten times more potent than tetrodotoxin, which itself is about ten thousand times more deadly than cyanide! If you do the math, that makes this stuff a hundred thousand times more deadly than cyanide!"

"Jesus Christ!" breathed both detectives in unison.

"My references say that a lethal dose of this stuff for the average human would be about a hundred micrograms, or the equivalent of two grains of fine table salt! Now, here's were the cardiotoxic, neurotoxic thing comes in. Once it's in your system, it attacks the nervous system very quickly, permanently shutting things down leading to cardiac arrest and associated problems." He paused a moment, then added "To make things worse, it's irreversible, there's no antidote . . . thus the phrase 'permanently shutting things down'".

Both detectives were making notes, scarcely believing what Alan was telling them.

Pete spoke first. "This would help explain the second death, why it reacted so fast. How the hell do you spell that Alan? I'll pass this on to our lab people, give them a head's up on something to look for."

Neil shook his head, realizing the case had just taken another bizarre turn. "Which still begs the question, why?" he asked.

CHAPTER 7

Two days later, Jake was still asking 'why?' as a jumbo jet gently carried him along at 38,000 feet across the Atlantic. Sipping a cold drink after a great meal, he stretched out his six-one frame, enjoying the space and luxury of flying first class. "I really could get used to this", he thought, momentarily forgetting the reason he was there. It was still only three years after he had sold his company and became independently wealthy, so travelling in such comfort was still a pleasant novelty to him.

"Why, indeed?" he thought again as he relished the closing movement of a Mozart symphony in his earphones. "Why would anyone want to kill Heinrich? What was so important about his paper that someone wanted to halt it . . . even destroy it?"

These and other questions still had no answers a few hours later as the jet touched down at the Zürich International Airport at Kloten, seven miles north of the city. With only a small carry-on bag, Jake didn't have to waste time waiting for luggage, heading directly through passport control and out into the airport. Looking around slowly, he absorbed the atmosphere and ambience that he missed when he was away from Europe. Although quite modern, Zürich airport had still retained enough of a European flavour to trigger old memories in Jake and recall much of his foreign service training. Of his seven years in the service, Jake had spent half of it in Europe, learning the language, customs and culture of several countries. Although Jake was trained as a field agent, his expertise in communications and computers restricted him to specialized projects. After Europe, he was then transferred to South America and eventually to the Orient, absorbing even more language and culture as well as specializing in martial arts.

He smiled to himself, enjoying the comfortable feeling of being back in Europe. He gripped his cane firmly and walked straight over to the parking valet service to claim Heinrich's car. He had learned during further discussions with Helga that it was her car, not Heinrich's. From what she had told Jake, Heinrich had not owned a car since his wife was killed in their car eight years ago. Like many Europeans, he decided he didn't need a car as he travelled so much by public transportation. He was often out of the country, or was lecturing in Munich or another city where a car was not an asset.

Although Helga had forewarned him, the little yellow Volkswagen came as a surprise, and Jake looked forward to driving it as he threw his bag in the back seat and climbed in. After a little familiarization, he was soon speeding down the N1 autobahn towards Winterthur and St. Gallen. The green Swiss countryside spread out around him as he raced along through rolling hills. In less than two hours he had reached the shores of the Bodensee and within a few minutes he left the highway to work his way across the Rhine to Bregenz. Thoroughly impressed with the little car, Jake pulled in beside Helga's house in just over two and one half hours from his arrival at Zürich airport.

After a sorrowful reunion with Helga, Jake joined her for lunch. It gave them both a chance to vent their grief and discuss what they both knew about Heinrich, and why he was killed.

"*Aber, Ich verstehe nicht* . . . But, I don't understand," Helga was saying as they enjoyed some fresh brewed European coffee. "I thought . . . I was told he had a heart attack. Now you are telling me he was poisoned?"

Jake could not think of a gentle way to put it, He knew Helga had been close to her brother all their lives, and even closer since Heinrich had lost his wife.

"I'm sorry Helga, that's what it looked like at first . . . his running . . . when he was brought into the hospital, all symptoms pointed to a heart problem. We're not positive, but we think someone put something in his drinking water . . . something that caused a cardiac arrest several minutes later, with all the right symptoms. It wasn't until they became suspicious during the autopsy. They're still doing some extra toxicology tests." he added, not wanting to tell her anything to disturb her further."

"But what . . .?"

"I'm not sure what it was . . . something very potent, a few more hours and they might not have found it!"

"But why, Jake? Why would anyone want to hurt Heinrich?"

"I don't know Helga, it's the same question we've all been asking . . . one I've been asking for days. The only thing we do know is that it has something to do with the paper he was supposed to present in Vancouver."

"The paper?"

"Yes, the paper on global warming. He mentioned it to me last weekend after he arrived. He didn't give me any details, but I know it included some of the work he had been doing in the Arctic."

Helga's face became pale, her eyes widened.

"Helga! Do you know something about this?" Jake asked quickly.

"*Oh, Mein Gott!*" Helga moaned. "It's just like before . . ." she said, shaking her head.

"What do you mean, 'just like before', Helga?" Jake fired at her. "What was just like before?"

Helga continued to shake her head, moaning "Oh no, Oh no!" She finally looked up at Jake, clenching her teeth and bringing her emotions under control. "The calls . . . the phone calls. Heinrich got some phone calls . . . several times in the last month. Sometimes

I would take them if Heinrich wasn't here, and it was always the same man. Heinrich was always upset afterwards . . . I'm sure it was about the paper. Heinrich never told me much, but I finally got it out of him that someone did not want him to publish his findings."

"You said 'just like before' . . . what did you mean by that, Helga?"

"Eight years ago . . . just before he published that big paper . . . the one that made him famous!" She started crying, then stood up and walked across the kitchen for a tissue. "He got calls like that then too. Ingrid took some . . . that was before he lived here. She was worried and called me about it. Neither of us could learn anything because Heinrich didn't want to talk about it." She stared directly at Jake, holding his attention. "It was shortly after those calls that Heinrich released his paper. Ingrid was killed a week later in that car accident."

The implications finally dawned on Jake. "Are you saying that Ingrid's accident had something to do with Heinrich's paper?" he gasped.

"I don't know Jake . . . I really haven't considered that before now, it was a pretty bad time, as you know."

The words hit Jake like a hammer. Was it possible? Would somebody actually kill a person to prevent a research paper from being published? He had asked that question a thousand times during the past week, but now it took on an entire different meaning. He had never considered a connection between Heinrich's first paper and the death of his wife Ingrid. It had all happened within a week . . . Heinrich was still at the conference, receiving accolades and invitations for speaking engagements when the news came through. Jake had flown back home with him, almost as devastated as Heinrich. The funeral, the grieving process, selling his home and moving in with Helga, all occupied Heinrich's time and attention for several months afterwards. Jake helped where he could, but eventually returned to his own life as well.

Jake slowly reached across to Helga, taking her hands in his. "Helga . . . don't get upset about that, we're probably just over-reacting to Heinrich's death." He tried to comfort her some more, slowly developing a plan in his mind. "Can you remember anything about Heinrich's paper? Did he keep anything here . . .?"

Before he finished, she interrupted him. "But Jake . . . that's what the burglars took last week. They went through his study . . . all his notes are gone, along with his computer." She stopped talking, searching her memory for something. "As you said, it's got something to do with the Arctic," she said finally. "He's been travelling a lot during the past few years . . . all to northern countries . . . Canada, Greenland, Russia, maybe others. I'm sure it must be something he found there."

Jake tried to figure out what the Arctic would have to do with a paper on global warming that Heinrich had mentioned to him.

"Wait a minute," cried Helga, "Hans will know something . . . you know Hans . . . Hans Bader, at the environment centre here in Bregenz." She flipped through a little address book she kept near the phone. "Also . . . Professor Esslin . . . Carl Esslin at the Munich University . . . he might know. They've worked together quite a bit, and I know he went to Russia with Heinrich last summer to collect data. He might even have some of Heinrich's notes. He called me right after the news mentioned Heinrich's death. He'll be at the funeral . . . you can ask him then." She paused, then added "When you're talking to him, you can also ask him the name of the Russian scientist they worked with . . . someone from the Russian Academy of Sciences."

Jake copied both names and phone numbers down from the book. He had met Bader several years before during a brief tour of the centre with Heinrich. He definitely knew Carl Esslin, both from his days at the university and subsequently through environmental conferences and workshop sessions. He looked forward to talking to him again.

CHAPTER 8

A cool breeze drifted off the Zürichsee into the city as the late afternoon sun dipped over the mountains to the west. Kurt Landau's temper was anything but cool after a rather contentious encounter with his "employer". He did not like being called an idiot, especially by a woman! Ever since his return from Vancouver he had a feeling something was wrong, something nobody wanted to tell him until today. As usual, she wanted to meet outdoors and had picked Bürkliplatz, the little park near the lake where some of the tour boats docked. The location was perfect for a private conversation as there was just enough background noise from the lake and public activity.

A man in his late forties, Kurt Landau stood just under six feet tall, his thinning hair combed back, accentuating his broad forehead, rounded face and dark eyebrows. His eyes darted around as his head snapped from side to side, scanning the shoreline walkers for familiar faces. It was a nervous habit he had acquired each time he became agitated. After the meeting, the woman walked off, leaving him alone, staring out into the lake. He had instructions to stay in the park at least ten minutes before leaving, and he knew better than to try to follow her. Unable to vent his frustrations by walking, he became more agitated, his head jerking around even more rapidly, his dark eyes burning like a caged animal. Trying to control his temper, he reviewed the meeting in his memory, concentrating on the name she had dropped, Jake Prescott!

"You idiot!" she hissed at him, "This was supposed to be simple and quiet . . . no loose threads." Before he could protest, she continued "But no . . . rather than a simple heart attack, the police now know he was poisoned, along with another man!"

"What, but how . . . ?" he began.

"Not only that, they know who did it!"

He couldn't believe what he was hearing. When he returned from Vancouver, he was quite pleased with himself and expected appropriate praise from his superior. Instead, he had been met with a cold silence for two days, then a brutal tongue lashing for screwing up. He still had no idea where or how they got their information. Still confused. he resigned himself to accept the blame, as long as he learned how or where he had failed.

"You were picked up by security cameras in the hotel," she spit at him. "They even have a recording of you giving the water to Kohler!"

He shook his head, wondering how he had bungled that. He had been trained in the U.S. and had worked for years for the National Security Organization in Europe and East Germany during the cold war. After *glasnost,* he worked as head of security for *Sicherheit Steinbock,* a large German firm specializing in security systems. He could not believe he had missed something as simple as that . . . one did not survive if you forgot those kinds of details.

"But how . . . who . . .?" he started, his head starting to jerk involuntarily as his agitation increased.

"A Canadian scientist identified you." Landau cringed involuntarily, knowing the name that was coming.

"Some guy called Jake Prescott . . . whom I believe you already know, something about that fiasco in Germany last year."

"Prescott! But I thought he was dead! How did he get involved with this?"

"He's a scientist, idiot! . . . just like Kohler . . . they worked together years ago, and apparently he was at the same conference. After all, that's his home town . . . didn't you even think of that? I'm hoping we can salvage something here and smooth it over before he starts snooping around."

Landau remembered Prescott, a knot of hatred rising in his throat. Because of Prescott and his persistent meddling, he had lost the chance to become head of the huge Steinbock corporation and make millions. "Oh, he'll snoop around . . . it seems that's what he does." He thought a moment, a trace of admiration added to the hate. "And he's good at it . . . if he gets involved, he'll start putting things together, so you'd better have your house in order."

"Don't tell me what to do, you incompetent idiot!" she confronted him, "If you had done your work properly, we wouldn't have to worry about some Canadian playboy scientist!" She paused, visibly controlling her emotions. "First, we have to get you out of town . . . out of the country. Interpol probably already knows you're here in Zürich. I have another job for you in Russia, gives you a chance to practice your Russian - maybe you can redeem yourself. Your instructions will be at your hotel when you return."

With that she had left, leaving him alone in the little park with an odd mixture of tourists and the occasional tour operator. Another tour boat was just arriving, unloading passengers and preparing for another cruise out into the lake. He watched for a few minutes longer, then started walking along the Bahnhofstrasse back to his hotel. On the way, he stopped at his bank, one of many Swiss banks along the Bahnhofstrasse. When he finally got back to his room, his "instructions" consisted of an envelope of money, some plane tickets and a phone number to call once he arrived at his destination. It was always the same . . . no details, nothing written, no indication of who he was to see, or who was paying him.

It was almost a year before, shortly after his close call with Prescott and that Interpol guy in Bavaria that he first contacted this organization. Actually, they had contacted him. After a bloody gunfight with mercenaries and the law, he was ready for a rest. He planned a few days in Zürich to withdraw some cash and relax a bit, then a plane trip south to warmer weather. He never made it further than Zürich. When he returned to his hotel the evening before he planned to leave, a woman was waiting inside his room. At first, he was angry, threatening to throw her out. Then she started to tell him things, things about himself that he thought only he knew. This impressed him enough to listen more. What came next was even more impressive . . . offers of large amounts of money, tax-free, no questions asked as long as he performed little duties as required from time to time. They had obviously done their homework, something that Landau admired. In addition to the money, he was fascinated by the puzzle of who these people were, and promised himself he would find out. He had learned years before that if someone was willing to pay a lot of money for a job, then it was almost a sure bet they were making even more money.

The rules were few and simple, rules he found realistic and easy to comply with . . . until now. One of the main rules, one which she had stressed several times was "no personal vendettas". Past experience had taught them that someone with a personal debt to pay usually got sidetracked, started to get sloppy, and were too easily traced from their past association with their "clients". Landau had agreed and accepted the rule, thinking it would be no problem as he had settled all of his old debts. Until Prescott. He suddenly realized he would like nothing better than to have Jake Prescott in the sights of an automatic machine pistol.

Putting the thought out of his mind, he started preparing for his trip. Before packing, he went down to the front desk to settle his bill, telling them he would be leaving later for a late flight. When he returned to his room, he pulled a small kit out of his suitcase and went into the bathroom. A generous hairpiece covered his thinning hair, drooping slightly over his broad forehead. A small moustache was added and a heavy pair of glasses completed the transformation. He then selected a passport from a small bundle he had in his case and checked his new appearance with the photo inside. He smiled with approval, then finished his dressing with a clean white shirt, tie and a conservative business suit before he felt he was ready to go. After packing the few last minute items, he quietly left by the rear stairs, hailing a taxi as he hit the street.

CHAPTER 9

Lake Constance, or what Europeans call the Bodensee, is a large, beautiful lake about forty miles long and eight miles wide. It consists basically of a widening of the Rhine River as it flows from the Swiss Alps to the North Sea. The Lake is surrounded by three countries, Germany to the north, Switzerland to the south, with Austria occupying a very small portion of the southeast corner.

Tucked away on this Austrian shore lies Bregenz, a beautiful, picturesque little town. Built on the lower slopes of wooded foothills that rise gently from the lake, it is an interesting combination of new and old. Well known for its famous Summer Music Festival held in a unique floating stage at the edge of the lake, Bregenz offers visitors an eclectic selection of history, culture, food and wine.

Jake always liked Bregenz, its old town section with interesting buildings, its food, its history . . . but with a modern casino that added a little extra spice for times when the old culture wasn't exciting enough. When he was going to Munich University, he would visit Heinrich in Bregenz at every opportunity. It was during these times that he first became interested in environmental monitoring and air quality sampling. The Environmental Institute for the province of Voralberg was located in Bregenz, operating a network of monitoring stations around the province and in a section of Switzerland nearby.

Jake had decided to walk over to the institute early in the morning, to try to catch some people he knew before they got too wrapped up in their day, or headed out into the field for some monitoring checks. From Helga's house, he had walked down near to the lake and along Bahnhofstrasse, the main street following the lake shore. He turned up Montfortstrasse a short distance to number four, an impressive modern building with a sign in front that read "Umweltinstitute des Lands Voralberg", or the Environmental Institute for Voralberg Province.

After introducing himself to the receptionist, he was quickly shown in to see Dr. Hans Bader, one of the leading scientists in the center and an old friend of Jake's.

"*Grüss Gott, Jakob,* how are you! how many years . . . five, ten?"

"Eight years Hans . . . Inge Kohler's funeral . . . now it's Heinrich . . . you've heard?"

"Yes . . . some of us are going to the funeral this afternoon. *Mein Gott,* I can't believe it! Heinrich was in such good shape . . . put us all to shame, I can't believe he had a heart problem."

"Well Hans, it appears he didn't have a problem . . . from what we know so far, someone pushed him along."

Jake explained the latest findings and the latest suspicions. Hans listened in horror, shaking his head through the entire conversation. He got up from his desk, his brow wrinkled with concern as he paced his office floor nervously.

"Hans," Jake continued, "Do you have any information about Heinrich's paper he was going to present at the Vancouver conference . . . the one involving global warming, and something to do with the Arctic?"

"Sorry Jake, only the basics. Heinrich and I discussed it over a beer a few times between his trips, or when he wasn't at the university in Munich. Something to do with the melting of the permafrost and releasing more greenhouse gasses."

"Yeah, that's what he told me too . . . but I don't have any specifics . . . especially anything that would get him killed."

Hans walked across his office again, staring out into the yard behind the center. "Jake, you are in the business . . . you must know that environmental news or so-called discoveries are not always welcome."

"Yeah, but . . ."

"No, let me finish. What I'm saying is that many of these little gems we so proudly present at conferences are not just academic curiosities for the benefit and general interest of the scientific community. In most cases, they are appreciated for their information, their data, their predictions or practical applications."

"Yes, of course . . . I know that." Jake answered.

"Yes," Hans replied quickly, "but what you are not considering is that not everyone welcomes such findings. In these days of global warming for instance, even the general public rarely wants to hear the truth, certainly not any of the governments, and definitely not the industrial giants. To most people, the term global warming only means that we're going to get some warmer weather, yet at the same time, you constantly hear everyone saying things like 'why are there so many storms lately, why are there so many floods, how come the weather is changing so much?' They just don't get it!"

"I know that, Hans . . . you can't please everyone, it just takes a little while before everyone understands all the implications."

"That's not the real danger, Jake. You're a bright guy, how come you haven't figured this out before?" He paused briefly as he paced across his office once more. "Hans and I talked about this many times . . . I really think he had it figured out. It all started with the Montreal Protocol, then Rio, Kyoto, Beijing, and so on . . . each time all the countries get together, more promises are made, more targets are set, yet years have gone by and absolutely nothing has really been accomplished. What I'm saying Jake is that many of these scientific findings are not welcome by the industrial countries, and definitely not by certain companies who stand to lose billions if these findings are taken seriously."

"What are you saying? Do you think a company, or worse, an entire country would not believe the importance of this . . . not take it seriously enough to take action?"

Hans laughed, shaking his head. "Jesus, Jake, you are so naive sometimes! Take a look around you! Can't you see the money involved?" He paused a moment. "Take the oil industry as one of the best examples. In the United States alone, they use about 710 million gallons of oil a day! Every 22 minutes, they use up the equivalent to the Exxon Valdez spill. Just think, all the exhaust products from that oil going into our air every 22 minutes and nobody gives a damn!"

Jake nodded, knowing that what Hans was saying was true, and part of a large, world-wide problem.

Hans continued, "Don't you see the environmental confrontations all over the world every day? Workers, people in the street, activists, local hire-a-protestors, corporations and governments . . . they're arguing over the last stands of timber in your own country, arguing over some obscure field mouse or small owl . . . even a dispute over an unknown snail or fish can bring a multi-billion dollar construction project to a halt."

Jake realized his innocent naivete had once more clouded his judgement and analytical skills. Always the optimist, Jake expected the best from people, a weakness that had got him into trouble more than once.

"For instance," Hans continued, his tone becoming more serious. "Did you know Bernard Limoges . . . a geologist from Bordeaux?"

"No, I don't think so." Jake replied, cautious about what was coming next.

"Bernard was a great guy, but too much of an innocent . . . much like you Jake. He was doing some consulting work in the Sudan . . . he found out something about one of the oil companies doing work there . . . something involving the deaths of thousands of Sudanese!" He coughed slightly, his voice breaking as he recounted the story. "Nobody knows what he had, or what he was planning to do about it . . . he died in a plane crash as he was leaving the area. Very little news leaked out . . . I think there was something in one of the French newspapers, a small column about Bernard, his work, and how he died in a small plane when it crashed in a remote desert area . . . sort of an occupational hazard."

Jake couldn't believe what he was hearing. "But how . . . who . . .?"

"Bernard and I were old friends . . . we went to university together years ago. We kept in touch . . . I had some emails from him . . . nothing seriously incriminating, just a hint of what he was finding."

"What are you going to do?" Jake asked innocently.

"Nothing . . . I've destroyed the emails. That was six months ago, and I still live in fear that somebody might discover that Bernard wrote to me. I have a good life Jake, I'm not a hero or a crazy environmental crusader."

Jake understood what he was saying. "Do you think Heinrich's paper . . .?"

"Jake, listen! Heinrich's paper is not the issue . . . not specifically. If he came up with a correlation between melting ice fields, thawing permafrost and greenhouse gasses . . . so be it! What really is important is whom this will impact . . . who stands to lose the most . . . which companies will have to curtail operations or even shut down?"

Hans' statements and overall implications slowing started to sink into Jake's conscious thought. His own analytical skills had overlooked a much broader canvas . . . commonly referred to as "the big picture". As he considered the details in this new frame of reference, he started to see the beginning of a pattern, a rough outline of something that was even more sinister than he originally thought.

CHAPTER 10

A cool mist had closed in on the lake, draping the entire funeral scene in a sombre cloak of grey. Jake stood beside Helga throughout the service, providing both moral and physical support when the cumulative anguish of the past week finally descended on her shoulders. After the service, mourners stood around in small groups, waiting to talk to Helga. One person separated herself from the group to come over to Helga. Jake recognized her as the pastor that had given the sermon and eulogy for Heinrich. Jake had thought during the sermon that she was very pretty, and as she approached them, she reinforced that opinion. Helga grabbed Jake's arm, turning him towards the girl. "Jake . . ." she started "I'd like you to meet Sabrina . . . Sabrina Wagner. She's an old friend of the family."

"Oh yes" said Jake "You're the pastor . . . I remember you from the sermon."

"I'm not really a pastor" replied Sabrina "I'm just filling in for the usual pastor, as Helga said, I'm a friend of the family . . . this was a special occasion."

No more was said, as others engaged Helga's attention. Jake was shuffled along with the group surrounding Helga, and Jake was disappointed as he lost track of this gorgeous 'friend of the family'. He only recognized a few of Heinrich's friends from the village as well as some of his peers from several universities and research organizations around Europe. As if planned, the foggy mantle hung over the congregation throughout the service, only lifting again within an hour after Heinrich had been laid to rest.

Helga had invited a few good friends and some of Heinrich's colleagues back to the house for refreshment. Jake kept looking out for the 'friend of the family', but was disappointed. It gave Jake a chance to talk to Hans Bader again, as well as Carl Esslin from the university in Munich. Carl had travelled with Heinrich to the arctic on several expeditions over the past few years.

"Well Jake," Carl started over a drink in a quiet corner. "It's too bad it takes something like this to get us together again. It must be . . . what . . . almost ten years?" he asked Jake.

"Yes Carl, I think about nine years . . . nine very eventful years!" Jake replied quietly.

"I'm sorry Jake, I know you were very close to Heinrich. Also, I was shocked last year when I heard about Stefan and Christa . . . that was terrible!"

"You have no idea, Carl, probably worse than when I lost my parents." Jake shook his head sadly, trying not to bring up the details in his memory. "The worst part now Carl, is that it looks like something like that is happening again!"

"What . . . what do you mean?" he asked quickly.

"Landau . . . Kurt Landau! The same guy that killed Stefan, Christa and all the others in Bavaria last year, he's the one that killed Heinrich in Vancouver and is still on the loose!"

"*Oh Mein Gott!*" Carl cried aloud, "I had no idea!"

"Well, it's still not official, and not many people know this yet, but he was in Vancouver last week, and they are still looking for him now." Changing the subject slightly, Jake asked "Tell me Carl, who were the other scientists you and Heinrich worked with on the arctic expeditions? Helga said there was a Russian guy."

"Yes, Klebinov . . . Boris Klebinov. A very respected climatologist with the Russian Academy of Science. We took several trips together, both on our Greenland trips, and up north of Murmansk." He paused, a look of concern wrinkled his brow. "Why do you ask Jake, is there something else you are not telling me?"

"No Carl, nothing I can say definitely at this time." Jake offered, stumbling a little. "It's just that there are too many coincidences lately, you know, too many scientists we all know that are having too many accidents."

"I know what you mean," Carl said. "Hans and I have been talking about this lately. I suppose he mentioned to you about Limoges, Bernard Limoges out of Bordeaux?"

"Yes, he mentioned him . . . sounded quite upset. Did you know him, is there anything else?"

"Only briefly. We try to keep current with many of the scientists involved with the oil industry, or any other industry that is affecting the environment . . . which is just about everything, I'm afraid." he chuckled. "In any case," he added, "Boris spends most of his time at the university in St. Petersburg. I'll email you his address later."

Jake thanked him and they mingled a little longer, enjoying a few drinks and getting caught up on the latest in each of their lives.

Early the following morning, Jake phoned his office in Vancouver, catching them all before they went home. Shannon answered the phone.

"Oh Jake, I'm glad you called. Pete Johnson . . . you know, one of the police detectives that was here the other day . . . he called earlier. They have been talking to Jacques at Interpol, got the scoop on Landau. They've been trying to trace him in and out of Vancouver - no luck! According to the flight records for the past week, nobody by that name came in or out of Vancouver airport. They checked Seattle too . . . nothing!"

"O.K., thanks Shannon, that's interesting. It just means he's travelling under a different name. I suspected he would . . . nobody with his smarts and background would use his own name after that fiasco last year in Germany! Anything else?" he asked.

"No, that's it. I think Alan has been talking with the coroner's office . . . something about the details on that poison."

"Could I speak to both Alan and Peter now please?"

Shannon quickly tracked the other two down and hooked them both up with Jake on a conference call. Jake quickly summarized his trip so far, eventually getting to his suspicions about the deaths of the other scientists.

"Now listen guys, maybe I'm getting paranoid, but let's take a look at what we have. Eight years ago, just before Heinrich presented his first big paper, he was getting a lot of mysterious phone calls. Shortly after his paper was presented, his wife Inge died in a car accident. Last year, Stefan Schiller and the entire staff of the *Umweltzentrum* was killed. About six months ago, a French geologist named Bernard Limoges died in a small plane crash. Last week, Heinrich Kohler was killed in Vancouver." He paused, letting the others write down the names. "Think about it, gentlemen! Each of these people was involved either directly or indirectly in an important announcement, discovery or disclosure of some kind." He paused again. "Maybe I'm paranoid, but I think there's something going on here, something we better take a look at. Alan, you know a lot of scientists on the international scene, check a few of them, find out if anybody else should be added to our list. Peter, get on your computer, see what you can find with your search engines. I would be very glad if I come back and you tell me I'm just going crazy!"

He left his crew to do what they do best, dialling his telephone again, this time to Interpol in Lyon, France. Before long, he was connected to Jacques Manet, the dedicated Interpol officer who Jake had worked with tracking down Landau in Germany last year to the final showdown.

His voiced boomed over the phone. "Jake old chap, how are you?" He laughed before Jake had a chance to answer. "I hear you're still a loose cannon!"

Of course Jake knew he had been talking with the Vancouver police. "Fine Jacques . . . obviously you've already been brought up to speed by our Vancouver police detectives. It seems our friend Landau is still up to his old tricks."

"Yes, your guys Johnson and Hagen have filled me in." He stopped a moment, gathering his thoughts. "Tell me Jake, just how the hell do you manage to get involved with this kind of thing? Once was bad enough, last year. But now this, what the hell is going on?"

Jacques' broad English accent came across the phone quite clearly, especially when Jacques started to get excited. Jake always laughed when he visualized this jovial man with name like Jacques Manet, coming out with a heavy English accent.

"Well Jacques," Jake finally answered him, "I wish I knew. You've already talked with the Vancouver cops, Shannon said they haven't been able to track Landau either in or out of Vancouver or Seattle lately."

"No Jake, this Landau is a slippery character. After he disappeared in Germany last year, I never did believe he died in that shootout. We managed to pick up his trail a couple of times in Europe in the following months, then we lost him again. We actually haven't heard of him for over six months, until your little episode was brought to out attention. Of course, we expected no less . . . with his background and training, if he doesn't want to be found, it will be very difficult.

Jake agreed, then started to explain some of his ideas to Jacques. "You will probably think I'm crazy or paranoid Jacques, but here's what we have so far." He continued, listing all of the "accidents" he suspected. "Please keep in touch with my Vancouver office Jacques, my men are working on a few ideas, maybe they can keep you up to date."

"Jake, after working with you last year, I'm not afraid you're getting paranoid. What I am afraid is that you are probably right . . . and that scares the hell out of me!"

While Jacques was talking, an idea was forming in Jake's mind. "One more crazy idea Jacques . . . while I was in Bregenz, I learned about another of Heinrich's colleagues in St. Petersburg . . . the one he used to travel with to the arctic. I was going to email him for information, but I think I'll go to St. Pete to visit him at the university . . . might pick up some more clues on what this is all about."

Jacques said nothing for a moment, digesting this new information. "I don't suppose I really have to tell you this Jake, but be very careful, Russia is still a different country to what you are used to." He paused a moment, then continued. "I wasn't going to tell you this Jake, as you're a civilian - need to know and all that. We just might be one step ahead of you for a change."

"What do you mean Jacques?" Jake asked.

"Well, knowing the timing of that episode in Vancouver really helps us, as it narrows down the time frame we have to deal with. The good news is that using this shorter period, we can specify a period we can check for Landau's entry into or exit from Canada, probably via Vancouver airport. Knowing this, we are running a face recognition program on some of the arrival and departure videos and passport information over that time period. If we get lucky, we might nail down at least one of the aliases that Landau is using."

CHAPTER 11

St. Petersburg, once the glowing jewel in the crown of Imperial Russia, was now looking a little tired and frayed around the edges from more than fifty years of neglect and rough treatment. Major construction and renovation projects dotted the city, with virtually miles of scaffolding, netting and canvas covering some of the most elegant store fronts and building architecture in Europe.

Unfortunately, the city's old Pulkovo 2 Airport, just south of the main population centre, a brutal example of Soviet architecture, was not even in the same class as the rest of the city, looking more like a neglected industrial warehouse than a modern airport. *Glasnost*, *Perestroika*, and other political and economic changes to the Russian system had not yet brought Pulkovo 2 up to modern international airport standards.

Kurt Landau watched the crowd in front of him, an entire plane-load of passengers waiting in line at the passport control in the airport. His head constantly in motion, his eyes squinting and darting about, always watching, looking for a familiar face, a suspicious individual or something out of place. The heat and humidity of the packed room permeated his clothes, rumpling his cool demeanour and expensive suit. "Damn Russians!" he thought, "they never did understand the concept of air-conditioning!" In a country that was so cold most of the time, the idea of spending a lot of money and energy to cool off a building either had just not occurred to anybody, or at least not considered a priority.

His flight from Zurich through Frankfurt was uneventful, and as he waited now in the queue, he looked again at his passport and visa, performing the final mental changes into the persona of Ernst Gruber, a travelling businessman from Leipzig, Germany. Throughout his career, Landau had acquired many identities, being able to switch from one to the other as required, together with the appropriate language and mannerisms.

Before long, it was his turn. He approached and handed his papers up to the grim faced woman behind the glass. Not a word was exchanged as his papers were studied, scanned and finally stamped and returned to him. He continued to the baggage claim area to pick up his bag. Normally, he would only use a carry-on bag for a trip like this, but he knew that a travelling businessman would usually have more baggage, with at least an extra suit and other clothing.

He headed out of the building into the sunshine, and hailed the first taxi in line, and was soon heading out of the airport area and down Moskovsky Prospect into town. He tried to ignore the wild drivers and terrible condition of the streets as they sped into the city, only to be jolted into reality as a large pothole jarred the taxi. As he had not visited the city for some time, he noted the major changes and construction since his last trip.

Eventually, they turned on to Nevsky Prospect, the main street downtown, and was soon at his hotel. He had stayed at the hotel before, and liked the location as it was close to some of his contacts and had several great restaurants nearby.

After checking in, he made two phone-calls and then headed out to his favourite restaurant for dinner. He took his time over his meal as he had set another appointment for much later in the evening.

It was getting dark when he left the restaurant, a nice warm evening for a walk. A few blocks up Nevsky Prospect, he turned down a small side street where two classic old stone buildings appeared to be squeezing a narrow little shop between them. The entrance to the shop was a small, metal door at the foot of a short stairway, a little bell ringing above his head as he entered.

The atmosphere inside was ominous and dark, resembling the interior of a very old museum. Old paintings depicting famous battles from history studded the dark walls. Various weapons and old firearms hung between the paintings, many very rare pieces that would have attracted top prices at a collectors auction. Hundreds of remnants of the Soviet era decorated the room, hanging on the walls, covering the tables and counters. Old military hats, jackets, leather belts, badges and medals provided a variety of samples for the serious collector. Kurt had seen a lot of this memorabilia all over Europe in flea markets and junk stores, but he knew this collection was genuine, not just kitsch for the tourists. A glass covered counter contained more firearms, even older and rarer than the ones on the wall.

As Kurt stepped forward from the door, he knew he was being monitored. He had felt it as soon as he entered the room, and had no doubt it started even before he entered. He only had to wait a few seconds before an old man entered the room from the rear wall, his seasoned face suddenly creasing into a smile.

"Good evening Kurt, old friend," he started in Russian. "It's been too long, how are you?"

Kurt stepped forward to shake the old man's hand, answering in the same language. "Hello Alexei, I'm fine, thank you. Yes, it has been too long." Kurt thought back many years to some of his visits to East Germany and the Soviet Union when St. Petersburg was still called Leningrad. He and Alexei had worked together a few times on some tricky assignments. He managed to save Alexei's life and get him out of an impossible situation, for which Alexei was eternally grateful.

Alexei reached below the counter and pulled out a bottle of vodka and a couple of glasses. Nothing more was said as he poured two glasses of the clear liquid, and they both raised them up in a toast *"na szdroviye"*, to your health! They continued to talk for another hour or more, almost finishing the bottle as they reminisced about old times.

"Well Kurt", the old man started, "Perhaps now you could tell me what brings you to St. Petersburg, and why the mysterious phone-call?"

"Well, nothing too mysterious old friend," Kurt replied, "I have a little business in town and would like to be prepared for unforeseen problems. Hopefully, I won't need it, but I always like to have a little extra security," he said as he gestured towards the firearms under the glass.

"I thought so," Alexei replied, "I thought it might be that when you phoned. I have just the thing, I think you'll like it!" With that he reached under the counter again and pulled out a small cloth bundle, unwrapping it on the counter. "I know how much you like the Makarovs" he said to Kurt, "here's a little beauty . . . a Makarov PMM, with a twelve round magazine, rather than the old eight round one."

Kurt picked up the pistol, feeling the heft of it, checking the slide action and thumbing the hammer. "Feels much the same as the older ones," he said, "I can barely detect the extra length of the magazine." He asked a few more questions of the old man, and decided to take an additional box of 9mm shells. Money was not discussed, and Kurt knew enough not to bring it up, not wanting to insult his old friend.

"There's one more thing I'm looking for," Kurt added as he pocketed the Makarov. He mentioned what he wanted, but the old man shook his head.

"No, Kurt, I don't normally have such material in the shop, but I know where you can get it." He pulled out a slip of paper and wrote down a name and address for him. "I'll call him tomorrow and arrange it. If he doesn't know you are coming, you'll never get in."

Kurt thanked him again as he pocketed the slip of paper, had another shot of vodka, and left the shop.

The next morning after breakfast, he left the hotel in a taxi, heading across the city to the address on the small slip of paper that Alexei had given him. After a rather brief, conspiratorial meeting in another shop, he finally left with the small package he was looking for. He returned to the hotel, pleased that he could now continue with the reason for his trip.

Later that day, he called the university, finally arranging a brief meeting with Professor Boris Klebinov at his office. At first, the discussion was rather stinted, as the professor suspected Kurt to be someone from the press.

"I cannot believe Heinrich is dead!" he said sadly. "I was talking to him just over a week ago, before the conference in Vancouver." He paused, looking intently at Kurt. "What is it you said you do?" he asked, "Are you in the environmental business too?"

"No," Kurt laughed, trying to put the man at ease. "Nothing so important. I deal with conference, displays, set-ups for trade shows, etc. That's how I was in Vancouver at that time." He decided to use the same story he used on Heinrich, just a salesman for conference supplies. Kurt tried to assure him that he had only known Heinrich for a short time and he had talked with him in Vancouver, just before he died.

"He mentioned his work with you, and was quite excited when I mentioned I was coming to St. Petersburg on business. He suggested I call you and get together for a drink." Kurt paused for effect, his face turning sombre. "A suggestion I feel is even more meaningful now, since his death." He listened closely to the other man, hearing the words having the desired effect.

"Why not?" he finally stated, thinking of his friend and colleague. "You've come to all this trouble for my old friend, it's the least I could do. I'm tied up all this afternoon, but maybe this evening! Where and when?" he asked.

Kurt did not want to meet him near the university or near his hotel. "There's a little bar on Nevsky Prospect, near Gostiny Dvor . . . it looks like a good spot, easy for you to find and I can walk there from my hotel." He gave him the name of the bar, and they agreed to meet later that evening.

The bar was noisy, obviously catering to young people and tourists. Pretty, topless girls danced in niches along the walls, or around decorative poles in the centre of the room. Loud music played while laser and strobe lights flashed around them. Kurt found a table in a relatively quiet, protected corner of the room, somewhere they could talk a little. Boris showed up a few minutes later, definitely out of his element.

"My God! Is it always like this?" he asked, admiring the girls.

Kurt laughed, "I think we're both too old for this crowd." He turned and waved the waiter over, placing some drink orders.

They nursed their drinks while passing the time. Boris' concentration wavered from time to time as the girls approached their table, flaunting their assets in his face. Kurt found it difficult to keep the conversation going, knowing very little about Boris' friend Heinrich. After about an hour, Boris left the table for a few minutes to go to the washroom. Kurt took advantage of the time to pull out his small package he had obtained earlier. He was anxious to do this right and not leave any loose ends like he did in Vancouver. The package contained two small vials of rather dangerous drugs. One was *Phencyclidine*, commonly known as PCP, or "Angel Dust", a drug known on the streets to be hallucinogenic and neurotoxic. The other drug was a variation of *Benzodiazepine* or *Rohypnol*, known on the street as a "Date Rape Drug", with sedative, hypnotic and/or amnesiac effects. Both drugs were almost undetectable in a drink, and that the combination together with alcohol, would cause some very interesting and severe reactions within 20 minutes to a half hour.

When Boris returned from the washroom, Kurt had two large drinks for them.

"Well, Boris, just one last drink and I must get back to the hotel . . . meetings tomorrow." Raising his glass he offered a toast. "Here's to Heinrich . . . may he rest in peace."

"To Heinrich!" Boris agreed, downing his drink.

"Are you going to be OK to drive, Boris?" Kurt asked, a look of concern on his face.

Knowing the Russians, he knew what the answer would be.

"Of course!" he said, wavering only slightly as he stood up. "I only have to drive to Pushkin, just a half- hour or so from here."

Kurt walked with him out of the bar, saw him to his car and said goodbye.

The following morning, he watched the news on television. Apparently there had been a serious accident on the road to Pushkin, killing a local professor, Boris Klebinov, and one other person, as well as injuring four more people. The police said that alcohol was most likely the cause, as all were tested with high blood alcohol levels.

His work done, Ernst Gruber finished packing his suitcase, including his new Makarov PMM, glad he did not have to use it. He made a telephone call to arrange his flight to Zurich and prepared to check out.

CHAPTER 12

The morning after the funeral, Jake sat in Helga's kitchen, sipping his coffee while he checked his emails. Helga was handling her grief very well, once the funeral was over and all of the well-wishers had gone home, she now settled into her normal routine.

"Thanks for coming all this way Jake, I don't know what I'd have done without you." as she dropped a big plate of ham and eggs in front of him. "And there's more over there on the sideboard." she added.

"Oh thanks Helga, that's enough! I don't usually eat this much, you'll have me gaining too much weight while I'm here. As far as being here, don't even think about it Helga" Jake replied. "Heinrich was a good friend and you two had always treated me like family after my folks were killed."

Helga then smiled at Jake. "So, you enjoyed meeting our little friend Sabrina?" she said in a quiet manner, eyes twinkling.

"Why yes," Jake answered, not realizing Helga was playing with him. "She seems like a lovely girl, certainly a beautiful one!"

"Good, I'm glad you think so Jake. I'm thinking maybe it's about time you started dating again, or at least thinking about girls."

Jake suddenly realized what Helga was up to. "O.K. Helga, I understand what you're getting at, but please don't push me." He paused, obviously deep in thought. "But I must say, Helga, you have presented a lovely candidate to arouse my emotions."

Helga just laughed, knowing she had succeeded in her quest.

Jake stopped, looking at the screen on his phone. "About this Landau guy, we're not going to stop until we get that son-of-a-bitch! Our man at Interpol has been busy, found out that when he left Vancouver, he flew to Zurich."

"Can't they just watch the flights out of the city, watch for his name to come up?"

"Not that easy Helga. This guy is smart . . . knows all the tricks to evade detection like that. He didn't use his real name, flew under an alias."

"But how . . . ?"

"They're using some very sophisticated facial recognition systems. Each time he does this, if we detect him, then another of his aliases is compromised." He started punching numbers into his phone. "Excuse me, I have to make a call."

The email he had just received was from his colleague at Interpol, Jacques Manet. Within seconds, the connection was made, and the very English voice of Jacques boomed out of the phone.

"Jake! . . . I thought that email would catch you eye . . . I assume you read about our success in tracking our friend Landau?"

"Yes, great work Jacques! Here did he go from Vancouver?"

"Flew into Zurich, not too far away from you, so be careful Jake. We're still trying to find out where he went from there . . . he's one slippery bugger!

"Do you now have a name, another alias?"

"Yes, this time he was traveling under the name of an American businessman called Frank Kirby. His appearance had not changed much, so we don't think he was trying to evade us. I think he thought he was home-free when he left Vancouver, nothing to worry about. It will be different the next time he travels, he'll have heard the news about what happened in Vancouver, and who else is involved." He paused, and added "This means you Jake!

"I realize that Jacques, he'll be just as surprised as I was to learn he was still alive. You guys did a good job of covering that fiasco in Bavaria last summer, I guess very few of the details leaked out. Now . . . the cat's out of the bag, so-to-speak, all bets are off."

"Jake . . . further to that other discussion we had . . . our guys have dug out a little more information. I just want to check a few things and get back to you."

"Good, I want to talk to my people as well. I'll be here in Bregenz for a couple more days, you can get me here or on my cell."

Jake had scarcely hung up his phone when it started sounding off again. He looked at the display. It was Carl Esslin at the university. A little surprised, Jake was glad to talk to him again, as their talk was cut short at the funeral.

"*Guten Morgen Carl, Wie gehts?*" he answered the phone.

"Jake! My God Jake, I'm so glad to catch you . . ." He was obviously upset, barely able to talk.

"Carl . . . slow down, what's the problem?" Jake tried to calm his colleague, find out what was disturbing him so much.

"It's Boris, Boris Klebinov. . . have you heard?"

"No Carl . . .heard what?" fearing the worst.

"We were just talking about him at the funeral. Now he's dead!"

"Dead?" Jake almost yelled. "What happened, when . . ."

"Just last night . . . I just heard it from one of my Russian colleagues that worked with Boris. Apparently he died in a car accident, trying to drive home . . . very drunk, from the reports."

Alarm bells went off in Jake's brain . . . another scientist? "How much did you know him Carl, was he a drinker?"

"No more than anyone else. He could usually have a few, and manage the drive from St. Petersburg to his apartment in Pushkin, about a half hour drive." He stopped, then added "I'm going to check further on this Jake. There was another car involved in the accident, but some witnesses said he was driving like a maniac, very wild and aggressive! Doesn't sound like Boris at all."

Jake listened to this news, storing part of it away while his brain was processing other possibilities. Helga watched him, knowing that Jake was experiencing some very strong emotions, and listening to some very disturbing news.

"What is it Jake?" she asked as soon as he closed his phone. "Bad news?"

"Yes Helga, very bad. I guess I won't be going to St. Petersburg after all. Someone just killed a good friend and colleague of Heinrich's. It was called an accident, but I'm pretty sure it was another one of these deadly coincidences."

He called Jacques Manet right back. Jacques had not heard anything about the accident, but was immediately going to check into it. "With each of these incidents, Jake, your crazy theory is gaining legitimacy . . . and as I said, that scares the hell out of me!"

Jake wasted no time in calling his office. It was late at night, but he knew they would be interested in this latest news. He reached Alan first.

"Christ Jake! This is just what we were talking about, what we were afraid might be happening." He stopped, something on his mind. "You said he was driving aggressively and erratically?"

"Yes, that's just what Carl's colleague said was on the radio, or wherever he heard the news."

"Noooo . . . I guess not. I don't suppose we could ever get a blood sample, just to see what else he had in his system as well as alcohol?"

"I don't think so Alan, but I could check with Jacques at Interpol, to see if they can get any information from their NCB in Moscow. They might be able to check with St. Petersburg and find out." He paused again and said "I'll call you back Alan, I'll call Jacques right now to see if they can do that before we lose our chance."

Jake called Alan back within minutes. "Good call Alan, but Jacques is way ahead of you. He was suspicious about the report, so he has already asked his guys in St. Pete to check for other substances.

CHAPTER 13

Jacques Manet was troubled. He swung around his swivel chair and stared out at his view of the Rhone River, just below his window He could see part of the city of Lyon and the countryside in the distance, a view he cherished. He had almost lost this view last year when he got into a lot of trouble after he took off to Germany to work with Jake Prescott and that shoot-out in Bavaria. He was reminded in no uncertain terms that Interpol agents did not run around the country with guns, chasing the bad guys. Jacque's only defence was "I'm sorry, I decided to take a week's vacation and help out a friend. How was I to know he was involved in this?" Although his boss knew exactly the circumstances, he accepted Jacque's excuse and smoothed it over with the higher authorities. Jacques could still remember every moment of that venture, and still got excited about every action they took. His thoughts brought him back to the present, and the possibility of another 'Jake Prescott adventure'. He knew he would have to be careful, or he would be out of a job!

Another scientist dead . . . another too many as far as he was concerned! That Jake Prescott . . . he's right again! This young Canadian has an innate skill to see things that others miss. He seems to be able to link events and fact that appear totally unrelated and come up with a scenario that at first looks crazy, but usually proves to be correct. Occasionally, he thought Jake would make a good Interpol agent, but then revised his thoughts to disqualify him, as Jake could not take the rules and red tape required to process everything according to plan. When Jacques first met Jake last year, he was formulating theories that none of them would believe, yet he was bang-on! After several events like that, Jacques developed a healthy respect, sometimes even a fear of Jake's theories. When Jake speculated some wild idea, he had learned to listen and take it seriously.

He looked again at the report he had just received from the Moscow NCB. It was part of a lab report from St. Petersburg, part of the blood analysis on the dead scientist Boris Klebinov. Because Klebinov was a member of the Russian Academy of Science, they had managed to speed things up and have a copy sent to his Interpol office as soon as it was available.

The most obvious thing was of course, alcohol . . . lots of it! That wasn't the disturbing part, because high alcohol levels were very common in Russian traffic accidents. The interesting items were two other drugs, not normally found in traffic victims. The first one was *Phencyclidine*, commonly known as PCP, or "Angel Dust". Jacques knew that this drug was hallucinogenic and neurotoxic, and known to cause very erratic and aggressive behaviour.

The second drug was a type of *Benzodiazepine* or *Rohypnol*. This drug was known on the street as a "Date Rape Drug", with sedative, or amnesiac effects. Anyone taking this combination would become very relaxed, then aggressive and who knows what with the combination of alcohol.

Jacques knew immediately that this was not your ordinary drunk driver situation. He called one of his colleagues, a medical expert, to discuss the results, agreeing that someone must have doctored this man's drinks, doctored them enough to make sure he did not get home that night. Jacques knew that Jake Prescott would be very interested in this . . . Jake's lab people had expressed interest in doing another blood test on this guy. Now he could supply the results, starting to confirm whatever crazy theory Jake was coming up with now. Someone or some organization is systematically eliminating scientists. The whole idea was too monstrous to contemplate. He turned to his computer to email the result directly to Jake's lab.

Alan yelled out loud as he read the results in his email.

"Are you O.K. in there?" Shannon asked as she heard Alan's yelling.

"Yes Shannon . . . perfect! Jake was right again . . . someone's messing with our scientists."

"Our scientists? Who are you talking about?" Shannon asked.

"Well, not really our scientists, but our colleagues in the science industry. That bloke that Jake knows in Russia . . . it wasn't just a drunk driving thing that killed him . . . he was drugged . . . really drugged!

Shannon told him "Send that to Jake right away. He's still in Bregenz and he might want to show it to some of the scientists there."

"You're right Shannon, some of them even worked with this guy. Bloody Hell! Jake will be very interested in this." He paused a moment, then called Shannon again. "Shannon, call Peter, tell him we're having a meeting in the 'war room'. We've got to discuss this some more."

The three met in their conference room, not sure why Alan called this meeting. After they were seated, Alan passed a copy of the Russian blood analysis around for them all to read. "O.K., this confirms what Jake was worried about after his last call. This is just one, but there are just too many coincidences, too many suspicious deaths . . . actually, some of them not suspicious . . . they look quite natural . . . which in my mind, and I think Jake's, makes them suspicious! Are you following me?" he asked.

Both Shannon and Peter were smiling as Alan announced his fears. They agreed. "Yes Alan, we see what you're trying to say. It sounds crazy, but I think that's what Jake was worried about . . . and we all know about Jake's theories."

Peter nodded, opening a file he had brought with him. "I'm afraid you're right. Jake asked me to do some searches, just to see if I could find any other scientists who have met an untimely or early demise. Look at these." He passed a sheet of paper to the others. A list of a half-dozen people confirmed their fears . . . situations too 'natural' to be natural. "I don't know, maybe some of these are legitimate . . . but I'm afraid Jake's theory could be true, someone is eliminating our scientists!"

"But why?" exclaimed Shannon. "Why would anyone want to do that?"

Peter answered. "I'm not sure, I still have to check my facts, but in most cases, they were about to announce something big . . . not like a new discovery, but a new theory which could affect us all. Mainly affect the bottom line of big business!"

"You're right Peter!" yelled Alan. "That will do it! You mess with big business and you could get into trouble. Especially anything to do with the petroleum industry. Just think about last summer, Jake's encounter with those guys in Germany. That was all about saving money on fuel, which could have amounted to billions of dollars! That's a pretty good incentive to bump someone off."

"Yes," added Shannon, "that's what Jake's friend was working on, was going to present a paper in Vancouver. Both he and this Russian that was just killed, they both worked on some new global warming announcements from their findings in the arctic."

They all paused, looking at each other, at a loss for words. Alan recovered first. "I don't know if Jake is available Shannon, but can you arrange a video link with him asap? We have all these new toys, let's use some of them, I'm sure Jake would approve, and he will certainly want to hear what we've found."

With the nine hour time difference, they managed to catch Jake just after he had finished his dinner, and was delighted to join their video conference with his crew. "So what's up guys, this is great by-the-way, I'm glad we have a chance to try out this new system."

"You'll like it even more after we tell you what we've found."

"I got the email you sent on Klebinov's blood test. It certainly looks like they didn't want him to get home that night."

"Right on Jake, but we're trying to figure out who 'they' are. Who's calling the shots here and why? We think we know why, it's just who that has us stymied." He continued to explain their theory to Jake, and watched as he nodded his head, obviously away ahead of them in arriving at this conclusion.

"Great work gang! I think I'm going to try to recruit some help from the big guns. I'll talk to Jacques at Interpol again, and as some of your 'victims' are American, I'll call Bert Jackson at the F.B.I., or even Scott Anderson at W.B.C., I'm sure he would like another story to work on."

CHAPTER 14

The small car wound its way along the narrow road, weaving to and fro to miss the pot-holes and washed out areas. Tall trees on both sides of the road absorbed the sunshine, blanketing the area in darkness. The woman driving the car was smiling, thoroughly enjoying the dark, rugged scenery, a view which stimulated memories of her childhood. Dr. Dejana Babić was born in this forested area of the Carpathian hills of Povlen, where she lived in a small cabin with her parents and her younger brother. Most of her childhood was idyllic, playing in the forest with all the make-believe mythical creatures, down to the river to swim and fish, and going with her parents on the monthly trek into Beograd for shopping and treats. Her father taught at the local school, which guaranteed her early education. Her mother supplemented her education with her extensive knowledge of local plants and herbs available in the hills of Povlen and beyond. She showed which ones could cure, and which ones could kill. Dejana expanded this knowledge later in university, where she concentrated on Botany and organic chemistry. This knowledge proved to be useful in later life.

Each time she drove through this area, poignant memories flooded back, some good, others bad. The worst memory of her life was about this place. She was in her teens when she returned home one day to find both her parents and her brother slaughtered in their beds. Horrified, she staggered around the house, not knowing what to do. Who would do this? What reason could someone have to carry out such a horrendous crime. She still had no answers when she heard some cars approaching, accompanied by load voices. Something told her to lay low and hide, not sure what to expect. She slipped into a closet, pulling some clothes around her, but still leaving space to watch through a partially open door.

Two vehicles pulled up to the house, spilling out a half dozen drunken men, each with logo on his shirt or jacket, identifying them as belonging to the petroleum exploration crew that had been working in the area. Some went into the house, the rest went into the shed where some livestock was held. They came out with some fresh bottles of wine and brandy that her father had made. Dejana watched from her hiding spot, each face burning into her memory. They passed the drinks around, then climbed back into their vehicles and took off.

Dejana almost collapsed with relief once they were gone. She still trembled with fear, knowing that if she had been discovered, she probably would have ended up like her parents. After sitting with he parents for several hours, she knew she had to move on. Packing a small bag with the few clothes she had, she took one more look at the scene and went out to start the car. She had already learned to drive the vehicle, but backing it out of the shed and getting it pointed down the road was a challenge. Before long, she was heading down the little road towards Beograd. Her uncle Jovan lived just outside of the city, so it was the most sensible place to go. Jovan was devastated to hear about his brother. "Who could have done this? Why them, what have they done? Did you see anyone around?"

Dejana never mentioned about the men she saw. She wanted to deal with this in her own way, extract her own revenge, so Jovan had very little to report when he called the authorities. They went out to the site to appear to be investigating this atrocity, but very little was accomplished. For years, as Dejana thought about those men, asked questions, periodically saw them in town and eventually learned each one of their names, as they were in the same crew and often worked together.

Now, years later, Dejana still fought the old ghosts in her memory as she approached what used to be her family's cabin. Her only satisfaction was that out of the six men that violated her family years ago, only three were still alive. Revenge was sweet, but incomplete. She remembered the first of the men she caught up to. He was tall, quite good looking, with dark hair and a beard. Dejana was a very attractive woman herself, and when she was going to university in Beograd, she worked part time in the local bar. She took advantage of her looks whenever she could. One day, this man came in and sat at a corner table. Dejana went over to ask him what he was drinking. She could barely control her emotions when she realized who he was. She was calm, and she was prepared. She knew that one day one of the perpetrators would show up, and she had something for him. She had been experimenting for almost a year with the wild foxglove plants to develop a variation of digoxin, a concentrated version of a type of digitalis. When the man ordered a glass of a local brandy, Dejana smiled seductively and told him she'd be right back. As she poured the shot of brandy in the glass, she carefully added her small vial of tincture, almost indistinguishable from the brandy.

She placed the drink in front of the man, "There you are, big boy" she said softly. The man looked her over hungrily as he picked up his drink and tossed it back. She retreated to the bar and watched from discreet distance. She knew he would not sip this brandy, and she almost laughed as he tossed it back in one go. "There", she thought, "now we'll see who is smarter." It did not take long before the man was in trouble. After he started groaning and complaining about heart pains and difficulty breathing, she called her boss. "Gosh Boss, it looks like that guy might be having a heart attack, can you help him?" It was already too late, the man slid down to the floor, gasping for air, clutching his chest. She rushed over and kneeled down beside him, looking like she was trying to help. Whispering in his ear, she said "This is for the man, woman and boy you guys slaughtered last year up in that cabin in the woods. Die, you son-of-a bitch!" A brief look of recognition or remembering flashed in the man's eyes just before he expired. Dejana stood up, trying not to look too satisfied. "I think he's gone" she said sadly.

The next two men also came into the bar one day, as Dejana calculated they would eventually. Knowing she could not use the same potion again, it would look suspicious to have two more people die of heart attacks when she was working. She was prepared again. The two ordered some cold beers with their lunch. "Perfect!" thought Dejana, as she poured another small vial of liquid into their beers. This liquid was another of her concoctions from the castor plant, which she had managed to extract sufficient Ricin to kill several men. The beauty of this poison was how slow it reacted. They felt nothing for a day or two, then would develop a fever, then vomiting, severe diarrhea, then seizures. Death followed shortly after. It was very difficult to track or trace to the cause, and was usually written off as a bad case of stomach flu or food poisoning.

Once the men left the bar, Dejana never heard about their problems until another worker mentioned their deaths a week later. Once again, she smiled and felt good.

CHAPTER 15

Detectives Neil Hagen and Pete Johnson were enjoying their morning coffee while they discussed their latest cases. Both men were intrigued and a little intimidated by the contacts they were recently exposed to. It was not often that they discussed details with both the F.B.I. and Interpol on the same day. And to think it was all driven by a local guy, some scientist they did not even know existed last week.

"Christ! . . . the way that Prescott described that Landau character . . . he must be one mean dude!"

"Yeah, and that guy from Interpol had pretty much the same opinion."

"O.K.," said Neil, "What, if anything can we do about it? We've solved some pretty messy cases in the past . . . what can we do here?"

"Well," answered Pete, "It looks like most of the action now is in Europe or somewhere else. What can we do?"

"What we always do . . . think it through. Our lab guy didn't detect any poison on the water bottle. What does that tell you?"

Pete thought a moment, then answered "The bottles were switched, so the poison would not be detected."

"Right . . . so what was it switched with? Did the perp bring along another bottle just for that purpose?"

Noooo . . . he would just switch with his own bottle."

"So it was halfway through their run, so that bottle should have the perp's DNA on it, wouldn't it?" said Neil, a big smile creasing his face.

"Christ Neil, that's why I love working with you . . . you come up with these brilliant ideas. Let's call Prescott's lab, we'll tell him too . . . what's his name?" as he looked through his notes. "Alan Cook".

Within minutes they were talking with Alan Cook. "Alan" asked Neil "Do you guys have DNA capability out there?"

"Yes, of course. Why, is the police department unit broken down?"

"No, but we have a sample we want you to run. We're going to have our guys run it first, and we'll try to get the sample over to you by courier. By the way, do you have a sample of this Landau's DNA?"

"Why, no, I don't think we do. There was nothing last year that was left to analyze . . . why, do you have something?"

"No" answered Neil, "But I think we might have. We just realized we haven't checked the water bottle for DNA. I know we've looked at it for that poison."

"You're right, we've been so wrapped up in the poison, we've missed the obvious."

Neil quickly answered "Don't get too excited Alan. We don't have any other samples to compare to."

"That's O.K., it has to start somewhere. I'll run it and send the results to both F.B.I. and Jacques at Interpol . . . see what they come up with."

As they finished their coffees, the two detectives felt very pleased with themselves. Another step in the long journey of detective work.

———ᄊᄊ———

Dejana noted the numerous changes that had taken place in the intervening years. Now, after many years of clandestine use, the building was a remnant of what it used to be, or what it could have been . . . a long forgotten Soviet project which never reached fruition. A little smoke curling up from a chimney was the only sign of life. Two vehicles were tucked away behind the building, under a large roofed area which served both to protect the vehicles from the weather, as well as from the prying eyes of surveillance satellites above.

Unseen sensors scanned the surrounding area, providing high tech security for those inside.

A stocky, well armed security guard approached her as she pulled her up to the front of the building. "Welcome Dr. Babić, it's good to see you again. Go ahead, I'll park your car."

She felt the warm glow of power and control as she tossed the man her keys. "Thanks Braco, good to be back." She watched Braco as he walked away, his muscular frame arousing feelings inside her. Knowing she would have to deal with those feelings later, she continued towards the entrance.

As she entered the building, she felt a satisfactory sense of accomplishment. She had taken the family's small cabin, together with the abandoned old concrete building and expanded both into a modern state-of-the-art biological laboratory. It was here she had developed some of her best creations, special poisons and hallucinogens that provided her with some powerful tools of her trade. Her trade? She rarely thought of it as a trade, but there it was. . . murder for hire. After disposing of the six men that had killed her family, Dejana felt the satisfaction of revenge, and knew she was very good at it. Surely there must be others who could use a service like that.

Her first 'commission', although unpaid, was a favour for her girlfriend, Svetlana. Her boyfriend had beaten her severely too many times, and when Dejana saw what was happening, she decided this man had to go as well.

The next day, she arrived at Sveta's place with a nice bottle of wine. Of course, her boyfriend invited himself to help with the wine. Dejana was very nice to him, telling him to go and relax while she poured the wine. Of course she and her girlfriend just had wine, while the boyfriend had some 'special' wine, compliments of Dejana.

Dejana had been working on this combination for some time and was anxious to try it out. It was a concoction made from Water Hemlock roots, concentrating the poison cicutoxin into a small amount of liquid she had in a glass vial. As she poured the boyfriend's wine, she added some of the special liquid.

They all sat around, Dejana trying to be sociable, knowing how much stress her girlfriend was under. It did not take long. He drank the wine quickly, as Dejana knew he would. Dejana obediently jumped up and poured him another glass. That to disappeared quickly. Before long, they both watched as the man started to get stomach cramps, then he broke out in a sweat.

"God, I don't feel so good." he moaned. He started twitching, then shaking uncontrollably. Dejana, knowing it was well past time for any help, moved closer to him and softly said.

"Well big boy, how does it feel now?" He looked at her, confused by her words. "I'm talking to you ass-hole! Now you know what Sveta feels like when you beat her! Nobody there to help. Nothing you can do . . . are you listening?"

"What . . . wha . . . what have you done?" he moaned.

"Just so you know, you've been given the cure for wife-beating . . . or girlfriend beating. I can guarantee you, you'll never do that again."

He then realized what had happened. "You've poisoned me?" he gasped. "Antidote, quick. . ."

"Sorry," she whispered back. "There is no antidote . . . but maybe if you hurry, you could drive into Beograd . . . they might have something that could help you." With that, he jumped up and headed toward the door. He didn't get far, he let out a choked scream and crumpled to the floor. Dejana smiled as he shuddered, then gasped one last time.

Sveta was horrified, yet quietly pleased with the results. "Oh my God, what do we do now?"

"We throw him into the car and dump him off the nearest bridge." Dejana answered. "This piece of shit does not deserve anything more. By the time he drifts a few miles down the river, there won't be any trace of what caused the problem."

She pulled herself into the present as she entered the facility, she pushed these memories aside, looking around and proudly admiring her accomplishments over the years. She had been correct, there were those in the world who wanted, even needed the services that she could provide. She learned that any time a large corporation was stymied by some obstacle, either big or small, it usually came down to one person, or a group of persons, or some ridiculous belief. Dejana found it very simple to eliminate the obstacle by hastening its demise, usually by 'natural' means. This meant that the individual might have a heart attack, stroke, or some other fatal failure. Sometimes it was an accident, things that happen all the time and nobody questions them. It was difficult to convince the first few 'customers' that she could help them, but after a few 'freebies', she managed to convince them to devise a discreet, foolproof method to compensate her for the services rendered. Once established, her prices rose accordingly. She tried to calculate what the 'obstacle' was worth to the client, alive or dead. She also devised a sliding scale, the price was dependent on the type of demise the client wanted . . . quick and untraceable, or slow and agonizing, so the client could enjoy the procedure. Of course, the entire event could never be traced back to the client.

The amounts became very large indeed, and in most cases, the obstacle was dead!

The next problem was advertising. This was not a service she could openly advertise in publications, media or on the net. It had to be very discreet, usually word-of-mouth. One satisfied customer mentioning to another the possibility of obtaining this kind of service. As she only needed a few clients or a few 'projects' a year, and the payments were tax-free, she managed to accumulate sufficient funds to expand her special lab and hire some very skilled and dedicated people to work with her.

The result was what surrounded her now in the Povlen Hills of Serbia. A remote, quiet little facility that bothered nobody, and contributed to the local economy as much as possible.

CHAPTER 16

Scott Anderson could not get Linda out of his mind. Linda Seymour, his fiancé, had called him earlier to let him know she'd be a little late for their rehearsal. They had finally set a date for their wedding, and Scott was more nervous about that than his involvement in some of the dangerous assignments he had covered for W.C.B. Linda was a sexy, highly intelligent owner of Seymour Laboratories with her brother Ed. Scott had met her the year before when he was sent to Los Angeles to cover what was labeled at the time as a terrorist "Gas Attack". Linda fascinated him from the start, a gorgeous, very sexy woman, wielding scientific instruments and knowledge of explosives as an everyday occurrence. While he was in Los Angeles, they became very close, and inevitably fell in love.

The so called 'gas attack' eventually turned out to be a government project that had gone terribly wrong. He came into the event late, but ended up very involved in the final chapter, which resulted in a brutal chase and explosive shootout at a remote lab in Bavaria in Germany. That encounter, although very disturbing and sad, resulted in some friendships with people he would have never even met, let alone become friends with. People like Jake Prescott, who some say was the start of it all. Not really the start, but the one who first figured it out and got him involved, along with the F.B.I. and Interpol in Europe.

It was odd that his thoughts turned to these people at this time. He must remember to check to see if Linda had invited them to the wedding.

As if on cue, Linda burst through the door, out of breath. "Scott! Thank God you're here!"

"Linda!" Scott yelled. "Of course I'm here. What's the problem . . . is something wrong?" he asked.

"It's happening again!" she said, anxiously. "That guy is on the loose."

"What's happening . . . what guy?" Scott asked quickly, instantly worried.

"The guy you were all chasing in Germany last year. He didn't die in that shootout, he was just in Vancouver last week and killed an important scientist at the conference." She was all out of breath, barely able to relate the message.

"Here, sit down . . . start from the beginning. Let's just put aside our rehearsal for now . . . he said with a grin. "Just tell me what you've heard."

Linda calmed down, finally cooling off enough to relate the news to Scott. "First . . . Shannon Hall, Jake Prescott's secretary called me . . . actually they were looking for you, and Shannon knew that I would have a pretty good idea where you were. She was right!

Last week, at a conference in Vancouver, a colleague of Jake's was murdered, just before he was going to present an important scientific paper. When they viewed some of the police CCTV tapes, they recognized Kurt Landau, the main bad guy from Germany last year. Jake's in Germany now, and they've discovered more events of important scientists being murdered. Jake figures it's a serious conspiracy to eliminate people . . . and of course he thought of you . . . just the kind of story you like to investigate and follow up." Linda was smiling when she said all this, but she knew what would happen, and already was thinking about how she was going to postpone their wedding.

Scott laughed, "anyone else . . . I'd say they were crazy . . , but Jake Prescott . . . I'd start to get worried, because he's probably got it all figured out." He turned to Linda "Of course, you know what this means, how'd you like another trip to Germany?"

Linda smiled. After the fiasco last year was finished, they had both taken an extended vacation in Germany, Austria and Switzerland. They had planned to do it again on their honeymoon, but maybe a little early?

"I'd love to." she smiled.

At almost the same time, Bert Jackson of the F.B.I. also received a call from Shannon. Even though she knew he had already been informed by Jacques Manet of Interpol, she wanted to talk with them both and fill them in on some of the details. She really liked Jacques, especially after he had helped Jake in Germany last year, pulled him out of a mess . . . actually then almost got him killed in that showdown. She counted Jacques as 'one of her boys', along with Jake, Alan, Peter, and the two Americans; the reporter Scott Anderson and this F.B.I. guy, Bert Jackson.

Bert Jackson was an F.B.I. Special Agent, a designation which authorized him to both conduct investigations and carry out arrests and whatever is required. Special Agent Jackson had distinguished himself in many cases, including the so-called 'gas attacks' of the previous year which involved cooperation with Interpol and other police forces in Europe. A tall, soft-spoken African-American, Bert made friends wherever he went, gleaning help and unwavering assistance from others. Shannon had only met him once, but she immediately liked him, especially after the support he had given to Jake and the rest of the crew. She was calling Bert now, trying to get him to fill in the gaps before others tried to explain what was happening.

"Hello, is that you Shannon?" his gentle voice came over the phone.

"Yes, Hi Bert, long time no see. I suppose Jacques Manet has filled you in about Jake's most recent theories?"

"Oh yes, he has. Normally I wouldn't get too excited about this kind of warning, but when I know it's from Jake, I get real nervous." He laughed softly and added "Your boss seems to have an uncanny ability to put things together, to link totally unrelated events to illustrate a conspiracy."

"So what do you think Bert, do you think he's right?"

"I'm afraid so Shannon. We've been pulling together some of these events ourselves, but they were just written off as unusual trends or coincidences. Nobody even dreamed it was part of a demonic conspiracy, a sort of 'murder for hire' type of thing. We'll know more once we pull together more data."

He paused, then added "I suppose you already know that Mr. Landau left Canada and is now in Europe?"

"Yes, Jacques was telling me that. I believe that now they will put a little more effort into the search, they'll find him. Jacques says they have been looking for the last year, but I believe they all thought he was dead. Now everyone knows he's alive . . . we'll get him!"

Bert chuckled at her comment. "Atta girl Shannon, you know we'll get him! So where's Jake now?"

"He's still in Bregenz, Austria, staying at his friends Helga's place . . . you know, the sister of the scientist that was killed in Vancouver last week."

"O.K., but next time you talk to him, warn him again about Landau. He landed in Zurich right after Vancouver, then disappeared again. Jacques' guys are trying to track him, but if he learns that Jake is close by in Bregenz, I'm scared to think about what he might try."

"I know Bert, we keep trying to warn him, but I'm thinking he wants to meet up with Landau as much as Landau wants him!"

"Yes, I've been thinking that as well. I'd hate to think what might happen if they bumped into each other on the street one day."

"Oh my God!" Shannon breathed.

CHAPTER 17

M arcel Bergeron had just left line thirteen and was walking as fast as he could towards his flat in St. Denis. Ever since he had moved to Paris, he used the Metro, finding it faster and more convenient than owning a car. There was no parking available close to his little two room apartment, so the walk from the Metro station to his place added a little inconvenience. When he first moved in, he didn't mind, it was just a little exercise which he sorely needed.

Now it was a more than an inconvenience, in seemed like a direct threat to his life! He kept looking over his shoulder, even though he knew there was nobody following him. That's not the way they worked. He knew deep down that when his time came, it would be unexpected and very subtle, not a direct attack on the streets. Ever since his last meeting with Dr. Babić, he knew his days were numbered. No matter . . . he also knew he could not continue on the path he had chosen a couple of years ago.

It had begun almost two years earlier when he was working in the Sudan. His daughter had been fighting a severe form of cancer, one that required a lot of expensive treatments, travel to Switzerland, Spain and Canada to see the best specialists available. Marcel was not a rich man, and before long, he had over-extended his finances and all of his credit, and eventually had to sell his home. His wife couldn't take the pressure, and finally left him.

Marcel never gave up on his daughter, figuring that a cure was 'just around the corner'.

Dr. Babić had heard about Marcel's troubles, and decided to take advantage of the situation. God knows how she found out, but that was what she did. Her own intelligence system kept her advised of any situations where she could reap an advantage or select a 'victim'. The term 'victim' referred to a possible employee to join her organization, the Sekhmet group. She had recently accepted a contract from a large petroleum firm to try to control some trouble-makers, specifically one French scientist who had been causing a lot of grief for the company, and subsequently costing them a lot of money. Something had to be done, and the upper management were not too concerned how it was done.

Dr. Babić eventually met with Marcel, after he had run out of chances and support in Barcelona and had moved back to Paris to use the big clinic in Villejuif, just outside of Paris. She picked a quiet day when Marcel was alone outside the clinic, devastated by the latest prognosis. Apparently his daughter would require more treatments, more expensive than the last, and he was out of finances and energy. Dr. Babić could not have picked a better time, Marcel was at a low spot, very vulnerable and receptive of any suggestions that might help his daughter. She started talking with him in French, first about the weather, then the clinic and the money-hungry demons that run it, then specifically about his daughter. She was good at what she did, and Marcel was defenceless, pretty much at the 'end of his rope'. When she got to the point where she mentioned a job where he could make lots of money . . . enough to cover this and other treatments, Marcel was interested.

"But I've already got a job", he said, a little confused.

"Good!" she said. "It's your job that makes this little project even more possible and perfect for you."

"I don't understand . . ." he stammered, "What do you want me to do?"

Then came the tricky part . . . where she had to convince him to put someone else in danger, perhaps kill them. She had done this before, so she knew just how far to go, what buttons to push, and when to back off.

"Some executives are taking a plane trip from your Sudan site next weekend. You'll be back at work there by then won't you?" She asked.

"Why yes, I have to head back tomorrow . . . I'll be on site for the next two weeks, then back here."

Dr. Babić smiled, knowing her intelligence gathering had been accurate. "Regarding that flight . . . it would be really worthwhile if they were delayed for a few days. It's quite simple . . . if the pilots came down with some stomach ailment or something that would delay the flight, then the goal would be accomplished. You, Marcel, are in a perfect position to make this happen."

"But how? What do you mean?"

She could tell he was confused, but not necessarily upset. She continued. "That's the same flight you take every time you come and go . . . so you know those guys, you have coffee every morning with them just before they take off on one of these trips. It would be very easy to slip something into the pilot's coffee . . . something that would upset him to the point where he had to postpone the flight." She watched his reaction, then added "What do you think?"

"Well, that sounds easy enough . . . are you sure this is the only way to do this . . . it's not going to seriously hurt him, is it?"

"No, it shouldn't. Pilots are good that way, they don't take chances, if they don't feel well, they won't fly. If he doesn't listen to these warnings, then it's beyond our control, not our fault."

She could see he was thinking hard about all the ramifications of such an action. "But what would I put into his coffee . . . what would do that without harming him?"

"Don't worry about that . . . I have a simple, effective, yet harmless material that is very easy to use."

"So why should I do this . . . what's in it for me?"

"That the good part." She said, knowing at that point she had him. She continued, explaining how she would handle all his bills for his daughter's treatments. "All your problems would go away . . . just like that! Sort of a tax-free bonus."

Marcel was hooked. He stopped thinking of the potential problems or legal ramifications . . . the only thing he could see was a clean financial slate, with the possibility of more treatments.

It had all seemed so simple when she first told him about his 'new job'. He had no problems the first time. She had given him a small bottle with some clear liquid in it. Following her instructions, he poured a little into the pilot's coffee that morning as they were preparing to go. He expected the pilot to experience some stomach problems and cancel the flight, but as the departure time approached, no changes were noticed. Marcel was quite worried as he watched the plane taxi out and take off from the small company runway. All he could think was "I guess it didn't work", and tried to put it out of his mind for the rest of the day.

It wasn't until late that afternoon that he heard the bad news. The company plane had disappeared and crashed on a mountain about fifty miles away, killing all on board, the pilot, one of the company executives and a scientist, Bernard Limoges. Marcel was devastated! He had grown quite close to Bernard as they worked in related fields. When he had said goodbye to him that morning as he boarded the plane, Bernard had reminded him of his plans to visit him in Bordeaux next year.

CHAPTER 18

It was more than a year later . . . Marcel had almost forgotten about his agreement with Dr. Babić, and his involvement in the plane crash. She contacted him one day and arranged another meeting. Marcel was very hesitant to meet with her, but then he remembered that probably because of this woman and their subsequent deal, his daughter was still alive. He felt that she should be given some time at least. As well, he found her to be extremely attractive, which helped to make their discussions quite pleasant.

"Bonjour, M. Bergeron, Good morning, Mr. Bergeron." She greeted him cordially. It was like they had been talking just yesterday, about nothing serious, not the disastrous events they had precipitated.

Marcel reacted accordingly, greeting her in return, ready to thank her and tell her the latest about his daughter. She smiled briefly, then continued talking, halting Marcel's account of his daughter's health. "I'd like to discuss another little job Marcel . . . something you should be able to handle quite easily."

Before she could proceed, Marcel interrupted her "Before you go any further . . . I was about to say . . . I am eternally grateful for the help you've given us . . . but I have to say . . . I am not going to get involved with any more of your 'little jobs'. The last one might have accomplished your goals, but it ended up killing my good friend! That stuff didn't work . . . the pilot didn't cancel as you said he would . . . he just took off, maybe that's why the plane crashed.

"Oh I'm so sorry Marcel . . . but if you remember . . . I said that we had no control over what the pilot does. A normal person would have stayed on the ground . . . but maybe he felt good enough to fly. I'm so sorry your friend was on the plane as well. All we wanted to do was to delay the flight." She watched Marcel to see his reaction, to see if he was buying this explanation.

"Whatever!" he cried out. "In any case, I'm finished with these 'little jobs'. Please don't call me again."

Dejana paused, thinking quickly. She had dealt with this problem before, but usually she had some leverage to make things go her way. In this case, the man's daughter appeared to be getting well . . . perhaps in remission . . . so all her advantage was lost. She would have to tread softly to gain some strength in her negotiations.

"Oh Marcel . . . don't be so hasty . . .the only reason I would ask you to do another job is that you are perfect for the job . . . working in the right spot . . . it pays well . . .and who knows? . . . you might need some help with your daughter again."

The last comment hit Marcel hard. He realized then how vulnerable he was to this woman's suggestions and 'little jobs'. He had to make a stand, or he would never be rid of her.

"I'm sorry . . . I just can't . . . I don't want anything to do with you or your organization again!" he blurted out.

Dejan's eyes narrowed, a thin grimace twisted her lips together as she tried to control her emotions. "I'm sorry you feel that way Marcel . . . but if you remember when we first met and you agreed to work for us . . . one of the rules was . . . nobody quits! Not ever! Once you work for us, you are on call for the rest of your life."

"What do you mean . . . the rest of my life?" he stammered.

"I'm sure you understand what that means . . . and it's up to you just how long that life is! Do you understand now?"

Marcel suddenly realized what he was dealing with here. He had made a deal with the devil, he had sold his soul, and could not back out of it. He quickly backtracked, appearing to agree with her. "O.K., he said hesitantly, I'll go along . . . as long as it's not going to kill people this time. But I am warning you . . . I am quitting. What is this 'little job'?"

Dejana realized that he had no intention of continuing their connection . . . something she would have to deal with on her own. "Don't concern your self now . . . I'll be in touch . . . and let you know what it is."

With that, she said goodbye and they separated, heading off in different directions into the Paris traffic.

He slowed down a little as he approached his flat. He knew he had some time. The 'little job' was not due to take place for another two weeks. He assumed that sometime between now and then, he would be notified of the details, and he would have to commit to acting upon those instructions. What could he do? Where could he go? He understood now why they had that last rule in place . . . sort of a "dead men tell no tales". They just couldn't have people who had worked for them and done terrible things for them running around on the loose, blabbing about their jobs. Marcel figured he had no choice, he could not continue along this path, and he could not just stop if he or his daughter were ever to have a life. He began to develop a plan of action by the time he entered his flat.

The first thing he did, after pouring a glass of wine, was to dig out the newspaper clipping of Bernard Limoge's death. For some reason, he had saved the clipping with others . . . small notices of deaths of scientists he knew, people whose lives were snatched from them all too early. He sat down to sip his wine and read through the notices. In most cases, they said that local authorities were investigating the deaths. Because of the young age of some of the deaths, the authorities were obliged to check the deaths further. Although it was local police who investigated these matters, the international police or Interpol were notified because the deaths were in several countries. That was what Marcel was looking for. He opened his computer and his phone at the same time. Within seconds he was dialling the number for Interpol.

It took the rest of the day before a cryptic telephone message arrived on Jacques Manet's desk. It read "Are you or anyone in your department investigating the deaths of some scientists? Specifically, one Bernard Limoges . . . last year in a plane crash?"

Jacques picked up the piece of paper, his interest immediately piqued. He quickly grabbed his phone, dialling the receptionist who took the call. "Annette, you dropped this note on my desk. Do you know who wants to know?"

"Well Jacques . . . he was very mysterious . . . didn't want to give out much information, but I convinced him to tell me. I remembered that name, Bernard Limoges . . . and how you've been looking at this guy and other scientists that have died recently. I really think you should meet with this guy . . . there's something about what he's saying that sounds rather ominous."

"Ominous?" Jacques repeated. "What do you mean . . . ominous?"

"Well . . . I know this might sound crazy, but I think this guy knows about who might be behind your 'murder for hire' idea. He's in Paris, only a few hours away." She paused a moment, smiling to herself. "So, when are you leaving?" she laughed, knowing Jacques' penchant for getting out of the office as often as he could.

Jacques immediately thought of Jake Prescott. "Damn! he's done it again!" thinking of Jake's theory on someone running a 'murder for hire' operation. "Annette, could you please call this guy . . . I assume he left a number. Then after I talk with him, get me Jake Prescott on the phone. I think he's still at his friend's place in Bregenz . . . try her number if you can't get Jake direct."

CHAPTER 19

J ake was getting bored, trying to figure if he should return to Vancouver. He had visited almost all of his old school-mates and colleagues from his university days, and it was mainly very depressing to hear about the number of those who were no longer alive. He promised himself to make sure all of his resources were put to work to solve this problem. His main target was Kurt Landau, and whoever was working with him. Jake felt he must have some associates or an organization that is assisting with these deaths . . . he couldn't be doing them all himself. The next question, and probably the most important one is why? What could be the motive behind these crimes. What reasons are driving these people? Too many unanswered questions.

Helga came over and kicked his chair to wake him out of his reverie. "Jake . . . here . . . get out of here and make yourself useful! Here's a grocery list . . . head over to the market and buy these groceries. With an extra mouth to feed, I've almost run out of food."

So Jake headed out, grocery bag in hand, feeling rather guilty. The modern Spar supermarket was not far away, so he walked. Limping along with his cane, he hoped the groceries would not be too heavy on the return trip.

He pushed his cart around the store, easily finding most of the items on Helga's list. He was nearly finished when he almost collided with another cart.

"*Oh, es tut mir leid,* I'm sorry . . . Oh, it's you, Mr. Prescott!" A beautiful young lady backed up her cart to allow Jake to pass.

"Oh no, it's my fault, I have problems steering when I have my cane. It's Sabina Wagner isn't it? And please call me Jake."

O.K. Jake, I haven't seen you since the funeral. How is Helga holding up?"

"She's fine, but this entire experience is starting to wear on her. We've found that some other colleagues have been killed as well as Heinrich."

"Oh my God! How . . . what is happening?"

"It's a long story . . . and not a nice one." Jake paused, taking a longer more appreciative look at this girl. Liking what he was looking at, he overcame some of his normal shyness and said "Say, Sabrina . . . I was hoping to meet you again one day. Would you like to grab a cup of coffee, or some lunch somewhere?"

She smiled, crumpling any of Jake's remaining defences. "I'd love some lunch, I'm starving . . . didn't have much for breakfast."

So they paid for their groceries and headed up the street looking for a place to eat. Sabrina suggested "I know a little weinstube over on Kirchstrasse, its a great place for lunch!"

So they walked over to Kirchstrasse to a building with a beautifully painted facade, one that used to be a hotel in past years, now a traditional weinstube.

"Perfect," said Jake as they picked a table outside and seated themselves. At first, they were both a little stiff, each one not knowing the other. Jake started "So, do you preach at that church very often?"

Sabrina laughed. "No . . . not really. I don't 'preach' there at all. I was just filling in for Franz Strasser, the usual pastor . . . he was home with a cold. He has many of his sermons printed out, and he likes my voice, so I just get up there and pretend to be delivering a sermon. Most people like it, and it helps him, so we see no reason to change."

Jake laughed. "Well, I must say you had me fooled. I thought you were a died-in-the-wool preacher when I heard your sermon. So what do you do normally . . . that is . . . where do you work?"

"I . . . ah . . . work at the tourist office . . . not the little one here, but the main Vorarlberg tourist office over in Dornbirn."

"Well, that's convenient, you don't have far to commute each day." Jake knew the little town of Dornbirn, a few kilometres from Bregenz.

"No, it is very convenient . . . but enough about me. Helga tells me you have your own business and are very good at what you do." Before Jake could reply to that, she continued "I hope you don't mind, but she also told me about your difficulties in Germany last year, and the friends you lost . . . I'm so sorry."

Jake had never heard someone refer to that disaster as 'his difficulties', but he just nodded and carried on. "Yes, it was a tough time . . . so many good people." He stopped, then added "We're afraid that was not the end of it. We think there have been other scientists, quite recently, who have been silenced. Heinrich was one for instance."

"Oh my God! You mentioned that earlier. What is going on Jake?"

Jake tried to steer the conversation away from the depressing thoughts of murder and mayhem and towards something a little more pleasant.

"So tell me about yourself Sabrina. You work in the tourist business, went to school in Zurich, what else?"

And so it went . . . quite calm and informative for a 'first date'. Jake could feel himself getting drawn into those beautiful eyes, and already wanted desperately to reach across and kiss those luscious lips that smiled so seductively. Jake couldn't help comparing Sabrina with his friend Christa from last year. But already his memories of Christa were fading. He had barely got to know Christa before she was taken from him. He started to think about how he could protect Sabrina from the 'bad guys'.

Sabrina was having similar thoughts. She barely knew Jake, yet was seriously attracted to him. As they finished their lunch, she decided they better cut it off before either of them did something embarrassing. "Thank you so much Jake, I've really enjoyed this. Do you think we could do it again some time?"

"Absolutely!" said Jake, not wanting to quit now. "I am sure we can get together again soon, carry on with our life histories or whatever."

They left the stube, both with groceries in hand, and with a quick peck on the cheek, agreed they would call and meet soon.

Jake hardly noticed the walk home, his mind whirling with dreams and romantic scenarios with this gorgeous lady. "Wait 'til Helga hears about this" he thought, knowing that Helga most likely already knew, maybe even planned it.

CHAPTER 20

Jake took the call after the first ring when he saw who was calling. "Jacques! Bonjour my friend, how are things down in Lyon?"

"I think maybe better than where you are Jake. I might have some good news . . . some justification of your latest theory."

"My theory? What are you talking about Jacques?" Jake replied, puzzled by Jacques' reference.

Jacques did not wait long or give Jake time to ask any more questions. "You remember? Your 'murder for hire' idea, the one we discussed last week, about all those deaths of scientists!"

"Of course I remember that discussion, but it was just a wild idea! What do you mean . . . you might have some justification?"

"Justification . . . proof . . . I don't know what you'd call it, but I've just talked with a guy in Paris who claims he knows who's behind all this . . . because he was involved himself . . . in the Bernard Limoges' death . . . the plane crash!"

"Holy! . . . you've got to be kidding! Who is he?"

"His name is Marcel Bergeron . . . he was a friend of Limoges . . . worked for the same company on that project in the Sudan. . . . I checked . . . the guy's legitimate, he knows a lot of information that was not released at the time . . . plus, he does work for the company"

"So what now? Are you going to Paris to talk with this guy?"

"No Jake, you know I'm not supposed to be doing things like that . . . I'm with Interpol . . . we just pass on the leads to the local Sûreté and let them handle it. Just thought you'd like to know ahead of time."

Jake heard what Jacques was saying, but did not believe a word. Of course he knew that Interpol agents did not go into the field to chase bad guys. When Jake had first met Jacques the previous year, it was in the field . . . Jacques had managed to track Jake down in a hospital in Germany, after he was wounded in a shoot-out with mercenaries on a river barge. Jacques had explained to his superiors that he decided to take some vacation, to look up an old friend. Nevertheless, he ended up in a lot of trouble because of it. Now, he was acting like his phone was tapped and everything he said was being recorded. Jake decided to go along with the deception.

"O.K. Jacques, thanks for the heads-up. I'll contact my office in Paris, and maybe they can talk with him."

Jacques knew that Jake did not have a Paris office, but assumed that Jake would be heading in that direction immediately. "O.K. Jake, I'll text you the information."

As soon as he hung up, Jacques quickly typed out a text message for Jake. "**Marcel lives somewhere in St Denis, won't say where. I am arriving at Gare de Lyon soonest. We'll all meet tomorrow at a little cafe near Musée d'Orsay. Marcel will let us know the specific location . . . be prepared to meet there about noon, but call me as soon as you get to Paris.**"

Dr. Dejana Babić hung up her phone after being brought up to speed. She was glad she had Mila listen in and recorded all of Marcel's calls since she had seen him last. Just in time . . . immediately after she had met with him, he had returned home and called Interpol, that so-called agent that had interfered with part of her operation last year and almost got Kurt Landau killed. She could feel her blood pressure rise . . . damn amateurs! Meddling in her business! During their conversation, she realized she would not be able to salvage this operator, so she would have to silence him. She immediately called Mila back.

Mila Dumont, the woman in Paris receiving the call understood right away. Dejana did not have to explain much. "As you can see, he is beyond help, and must be silenced. Can you handle it?"

"Yes of course . . . I still have enough of that 'special medicine' left over from the last job. Should be enough for a spectacular heart attack. How do you want it, slow or quick?"

"Please, nothing spectacular, but you'd better make it quick . . . if he has a meeting set up already . . . somewhere near Musée d'Orsay, we just have to wait to find out exactly where. The 'special medicine' that Mila referred to was a concentrated extract of digitalis from Dejana's special lab in Serbia, guaranteed to bring on a fatal heart attack within minutes of drinking it. Will you have enough time to get there after you find out?"

"Yes, of course. Any calls or texts he sends or receives on his phone are duplicated on mine. I'll just make sure I am near Musée d'Orsay in the morning, and we'll take it from there. There are a lot of little cafes and bistros near the Musée, that's most likely where they would meet."

"Excellent! This is important . . . we can't have this guy blabbing a lot of information to Interpol or the local flics."

Jake called his office to inform them of his progress. He texted some messages to Shannon and asked her to pass the information about Marcel Bergeron to Alan and Peter. They might be able to dig out more details on the net, or at least find out where he lives. He then checked a few details on his phone. "Helga," he said as they were finishing lunch, "I might have to borrow your car again. I'm going to catch the next train from Zurich to Paris. I have to be in Paris before noon tomorrow."

"No problem Jake," she laughed, already getting used to his crazy, last minute decisions.

"This is important, Helga. I think we'll be meeting with a man that knows who is arranging all of these 'unfortunate accidents', or early heart attacks."

"Oh my God, Jake! Of course you can use the car. I never use it . . . it was Heinrich's car, he loved that little Volkswagen."

Jake headed off to his room to pack his gear and leave immediately. Already he could feel the excitement of the hunt, the same feeling he remembered from last summer, when they were following the people who had kidnapped his old friend and mentor, the chase that ended in a shootout with terrorists and mercenaries that killed his friend, his lover, and destroyed a research facility in southern Germany. He composed himself as he said goodbye to Helga and left the house. "I've got this 'smart phone' now Helga, so you can call or text me any time." He laughed at himself as his friends and staff had all had kidded him about not using his phone enough. He slowly started to feel calmer as he sped down the highway in Helga's little yellow Volkswagen, thinking about his moves for the next twenty-four hours.

CHAPTER 21

The drive back to Zurich gave Jake ample time to review his memories of his lunch with Sabrina. In one way he felt a little guilty . . . he knew he had loved Christa, even though he never got to tell her before she was taken from him. The memory still hurt, bringing tears to his eyes when he recalled their encounters. But Sabrina was . . . was . . . he couldn't really put it in words. He only knew that she had made a big impression on his emotions, and she was an exciting change in his life that he looked forward to dealing with once he returned to Bregenz. Return to Bregenz . . . a move he had not really planned . . . to spend much more time there, but he could see now that he must . . . he must see her again and declare his feelings for her before it was too late.

The time passed quickly and before long, he was on the TGV train to Paris. TGV – *train à grand vitesse,* or high speed train, the designation for several of the high speed trains in France. This one was called the TGV Lyria, travelling over three hundred kilometres per hour, it only takes just over four hours to get to Paris from Zurich. Jake loved the European trains, especially these fast ones, much faster than flying, considering the time to and from airports.

He sat back in the dining car, enjoying a nice Côte de Rhône wine with his meal. As the landscape swiftly went by the windows, he said to himself 'why are you here? What are you trying to prove? This is not your job . . . leave it up to the law enforcement people, the gendarmes, Sûreté, or people like Jacques in Interpol.' Logically, he could almost convince himself to leave it alone, but emotionally, he could not! He felt an uncontrollable impulse, a drive to finish this, to avenge the deaths of his friends, to stop this crazy, dangerous situation from continuing. He tried to figure out what kind of organization or even what kind of individual runs a "murder for hire" business. It all sounded so bizarre, but after his experience from last year, he realized that if there was enough money involved, there would always be someone there to provide the service. He tried to reach Jacques, knowing that he too was most likely on a train heading for Paris. Failing that, he called his office, loving the fact that he could call anyone he wanted. He remembered the time in the past when he would have to use a pay-phone/land-line, which was not always convenient or even possible. Shannon answered right away, excited to hear that Jake was traveling through France at over three hundred kilometres per hour. "Oh Jake, I wish I were with you now, I've never been to France."

"Believe me Shannon, although this is a great way to get from one spot to another, it is not a great way to see France . . . or any other country. You want to travel slow and easy, there are many other ways to see the country."

"Oh maybe some day . . ." she mused. "Before I forget, Bert Jackson from the F.B.I. called. I think he's been talking with Jacques Manet and wants to talk to you . . . especially after he heard why you're going to Paris."

"O.K. Shannon, thanks. I'll call him as soon as we finish our meeting with this guy and know what's going on. I'll talk to you later, probably tomorrow some time." As Jake hung up his phone, he made a note to take his staff on a European trip one day, give them all a treat. He could afford it, and they certainly deserved it.

———ⱲⱲⱲ———

Kurt Landau was angry again, angry with himself and angry with that Serbian bitch that just chewed him out again. He couldn't believe that the authorities in St. Petersburg had checked Boris' blood and found the extra drugs he had given him that evening. Normally, there were drunken drivers all over Russia, with many of them involved in accidents, almost daily. Even serious accidents causing deaths are not always scrutinized, especially if the driver's blood-alcohol is extremely high, there is very little reason to look for more drugs, an overdose of alcohol is usually sufficient.

Once the authorities learned of this, more attention was being paid to his associates, his visitors, and his past associates. When Dr. Babić learned about this, she blamed Kurt for allowing such a thing to happen.

"But I have no control over what tests they run!" he pleaded. He could not think of a situation that would require these extra tests, tests that cost extra money . . . why?

"You should have used something that is not so detectable, not so obvious." She paused a moment then added "It's that damn Interpol guy . . . Jacques Manet . . . and that damn amateur scientist Prescott from Canada! I think they triggered the extra tests."

Kurt could not believe what she was saying. "What . . . how in hell . . . where did you get that information?"

"Never mind where I got it! I know that you and that Canadian have some history, so you know how troublesome he can be." She stopped, then added "And that damn Interpol agent . . . I can't understand what the hell he's doing running around interfering with our work!"

Kurt could feel his blood pressure rising. Jake Prescott! Again! He thought carefully about what he was going to say next. "Dr. Babić, I know your rules do not allow for personal vendettas, but I must plead that this is a special case. Not only is this personal, but this guy must be eliminated before he brings us down . . . brings you down!" He added the last part to drive home to her that something has to be done.

He could almost hear her thoughts over the phone. There was a long pause. "Dr. Babić . . . are you still there?"

Finally, an answer came back . . . the words he was hoping for. "Yes, I must agree with you Kurt . . . he must be stopped . . . by whatever means!"

Kurt could feel his blood pressure drop slightly as a feeling of satisfaction started within him. At last, he was going to be able to get even with that damn Canadian . . . and actually get paid for it! As for the Interpol guy . . . he would worry about him later . . . first things first.

CHAPTER 22

The next day was warm and sunny. The visitors were filling the Paris streets as soon as the sun began to light up all the tourist attractions. Near the Musée d'Orsay, many of the side-streets were already crowded, the sidewalk cafes and little bistros already bustling with both the local workers and visitors enjoying their cafe-au-lait and croissants.

Jacques Manet and Jake Prescott added to this throng, eventually arriving at Place Saint André des Arts, a little pretty little square under some lovely shade trees. It was filled with popular cafes and bistros, and they found the one they had agreed upon. They were enjoying a coffee at a little sidewalk table, trying to look as natural as possible and non-threatening as they waited for their man to arrive at their rendez-vous. An enterprising youth was wandering around, peddling postcards and small souvenirs, while a woman was going from table to table taking photos of tourists as they enjoyed the Paris ambience.

A man approached them, cautiously at first, then realizing who they were, he came over and joined them at their table.

"Marcel Bergeron, I presume?" Jacques asked.

"*Oui,* yes, and you are Jacques Manet? I recognize you from the newspaper clipping from last year . . . but who is this? You did not tell me you were bringing another person."

Jacques introduced Jake and explained why he was there, and a quick review of the events from the previous year, and Jake's involvement in them. He seemed to understand the connection and proceeded to tell a little bit about himself and how he first got involved. Although they felt sympathetic to the man's concern over his daughter, they really wanted him to get to the 'meat' of the situation . . . who, what, and why.

Marcel explained his involvement, how he had been approached by this Dr. Babić of the Sekhmet organization to doctor the pilot's coffee. The pilot was only supposed to get an upset stomach and delay the flight, but it turned into something more serious and the plane crashed. He explained how he got paid, very large sums that helped pay for his daughter's treatments. He then went on to describe some of the 'ground rules' that she had about no personal vendettas and no quitting. They were interrupted by the waiter who brought another coffee and then left them to talk.

Meanwhile the woman taking photos was getting very close, taking a photo of the group at the next table. Soon she was at their table, showing them some lovely souvenir photos, both posed and candid. They suspended their talk while the photographer was giving her sales pitch. Realizing they were not going to get rid of her easily, they agreed to buy some photos. Jake whispered over to Jacques that they could use a good photo of Marcel, even though they had already taken some with their phones.

The woman proceeded to compose the photo, trying several angles to include the bistro in the background, watching the angle of the light, and what was on the table. She came over and shuffled some of the cups and plates around, careful not to get them mixed up, then stood back and took several shots. She had a small printer in her case, and within minutes, handed them some lovely photos of their little rendez-vous. They paid her, and with a quick "Merci", she disappeared into the crowd.

"I guess she's finished for the day," Jake said, thinking there were a lot more tourists that she could approach. The photo was very good quality and she could have sold many more.

Their discussion continued, and just before they were going to order another coffee, Marcel started to sweat and have difficulty breathing. "Are you O.K.?" asked Jacques. "You don't look so good."

"No, I don't feel very good." he answered, clutching his chest. His eyes became wide, obviously terrified, *"Mon Dieu!* She's got to me, I thought I was safe."

"What do you mean?" asked Jake, already suspecting what had happened.

"Please, quick! Call an ambulance, medic, doctor . . . I've been poisoned!" With that, he slowly slid off his chair down to the ground.

Jacques was already on the phone, calling for help. "Jake! Where's that photo-girl? She must have done something!" He looked at the little table with the three cups. "And make sure our waiter doesn't disappear! Don't get those cups mixed up, and hang onto them."

Jake jumped up and tried to spot the girl who had just left their table. She was nowhere in sight. "That's why she didn't stick around." he muttered. As he turned around, Jacques was already performing C.P.R. on Marcel.

When the medics arrived, they continued with the C.P.R. as they carted him off. They took Marcel to the nearest hospital, but it was too late. Initial diagnosis indicated a massive heart attack.

It was past noon when they finally got clear of the authorities. Jake's presence was easy enough to explain, he was just another Canadian tourist enjoying the sights of Paris. The presence of an Interpol agent on the streets of Paris was a little harder to explain, especially to some officers of the local Sûreté. Jacques just had to plead innocence and said he was just showing Jake some of the sights. Their meeting was explained as an intelligence gathering meeting from a police informant. Their proximity to Marcel Bergeron while he was being poisoned was a little harder to explain. Jacques had to fill them in a little about his investigation and try to get them to keep it under their hats, so-to-speak. He made sure they would test both the remaining coffees and Marcel's stomach contents for toxic materials.

When they explained their suspicions about the woman photographer, only one cop was familiar with someone like that. "It could be Mila, I think her little business is called Mila's Memories. I've seen her before, she hangs out around a lot of the busy tourist sites . . . does a pretty good business I suspect." They did not know where she lived, or much else about her. They would work on that and let them know.

As they left their meeting with the authorities, Jacques and Jake were both very hungry and definitely ready for a stiff drink.

"Thank God that's over!" Jake exclaimed as they settled into a restaurant nearby and ordered their drinks. "Just what the hell went wrong there Jacques? How could we have been so stupid, so sloppy that we missed that entire job? Here we've been talking about the possibility of a potential 'hit man' in action, and we sat there, unconcerned, while she did her dastardly deed!"

"I agree Jake, I'm afraid we were not prepared for such a bold attack. The nerve, the utter recklessness of the action."

Jake answered "It could have been the waiter, but I'm pretty sure that girl slipped something into Marcel's coffee when she was shuffling the cups and things around on the table to compose the photo."

"Quite possible. I think she's has done this before and is very skilled, or . . . the conditions dictate that quick action was required."

"What conditions?" asked Jake.

"We're starting to see the pattern Jake, we've been talking about their business, checking into many of these deaths, deaths that were supposed to look 'natural' and be left alone."

"You're right . . . and that worries me. We've just lost a valuable witness . . . just think . . . if this organization . . . this person . . . is willing to eliminate people for their own ends, how far are they willing to go? Perhaps they are getting nervous, considering all the inquiries we've been making . . . maybe we are getting close. If that is the case, and they are getting nervous, do you think they might take some rash action to slow us down or stop us? Are we under threat, are our friends and relatives in danger?"

"Oh my God Jake, I hadn't thought about that possibility! Do you think they might try something to slow us down?"

"I wouldn't doubt it, Jacques. I think we should consider that possibility and be prepared."

CHAPTER 23

Kurt Landau had arrived in Frankfurt and was reading the information he had received about Heinrich Kohler, the man he had disposed of in Vancouver. He knew that Heinrich had lived with his sister in Bregenz, Austria, and were good friends with Jake Prescott. Prescott had been staying there after Heinrich's funeral. Every time he thought about Prescott, he could feel his temper start to flare, but he knew he had to slow down, think things through, and don't do anything careless. He did not know if Prescott was still in Bregenz, or had returned to Vancouver. It did not matter, as the revenge he planned for him included everyone who got in his way. He knew he could strike without Prescott even knowing who or what was happening, but he did not want that. He wanted him to know who was behind it, preferably face to face, so he could relish the experience, enjoy watching his arch-enemy suffer before he died. When that was done, he was going after that damn Interpol agent, Jacques Manet.

But first . . . he was getting ahead of himself. He rented a car and programmed the GPS to take him to Bregenz, Austria. When he stopped for lunch, he called Prescott's office and left a message. **"Mr. Prescott, I'm sure you know who this is. I think we have some unfinished business to attend to. I'm in Bregenz now and plan to visit some of your friends, just to pass the time, if you**

know what I mean." He then hung up the phone, imagining the response that message would initiate.

When Jake checked his voice-mails later that day, he recognized the voice immediately. He had only heard Landau's voice once before, the fateful few moments before the bloody shoot-out in Bavaria the previous year. Now it was Jake's turn to burn! He could feel his temper rise, the brutal memories return, and his thoughts of revenge cloud his judgement. Above all, his worst fears became real.

Across the table, Jacques Manet could see the transformation happen, the look of horror and hate that came across his face. "What's happening Jake, are you O.K.?"

"Landau!" was all Jake had to say.

"Where?"

"Bregenz."

"Christ!"

They looked at each other, knowing that what they had just been talking about was coming true. "Do you think he's involved with this Serbian bitch too?" Jake asked, knowing the answer already.

Jacques was on his phone almost immediately, talking with one of his colleagues in Lyon, filling him in with the latest news, about their meeting, then about Jake's call from Landau. The entire structure of the International Police organization received a jolt of adrenalin when they learned the whereabouts of Landau.

Jake wasted no time. He called a taxi and said to Jacques "I'm heading to the train station, catching the next train back to Zurich. I can be in Bregenz by late this evening if the connections are good. I wish I could fly, but that would take me too long." Jake was worried about Helga being alone with Landau on the loose.

Suddenly, he thought about Sabrina. "Oh my God!" he exclaimed, thinking that history could be repeating itself.

"What is it Jake, what's the problem?" Before Jake could answer, he continued "I'm coming with you. It's on my way to Lyon, and besides, we can keep each other company on the train."

Jake entered the numbers of Helga Kohler first. She answered almost immediately. "Helga . . . it's Jake . . . yes, everything is good. I'm going to try to get back tonight." He paused, not sure how he was going to tell her. "Helga . . . is there anybody you could go and stay with for a few days?

"Why Jake . . . what's the matter, am I in danger?" Helga was smarter than Jake thought.

"No Helga, I don't think so . . ." trying to sound confident. "But remember, those people broke into your house not long ago? If they did not get what they were looking for the first time, I think they might try it again."

He thought about Sabrina, and knew he must call her as well. Landau did not yet know about Jake's admiration of Sabrina, so there should be no danger there. But he could not take a chance . . . he could not take another loss of a loved one. He then thought of something. "Helga, do you know the Wagners very well? I mean . . . well enough to go a stay with them for a short time. I'm sure Sabrina would be good company . . . and you could watch over each other."

"Of course Jake, they are old friends, I'm sure it will be fine. You call Sabrina and explain."

Of course, Helga knew that something serious was happening. Jake would not suggest such an unusual move unless there was some kind of danger, not just the possibility of another burglar.

He then called Sabrina, hoping she was home and would answer her phone.

"*Bitte,* hello?" her voice was like a salve to Jake's nerves.

"Sabrina . . . it's Jake . . . Jake Prescott."

"Oh hello, Jake . . ." she started to laugh . . . "I'm glad you clarified which Jake, I know so many. How are you?"

"Fine Sabrina . . . it is so good to hear your voice." He stopped, not knowing how much to tell her. He realized she had to know the situation and the potential dangers. "Sabrina, I'm on my way back from Paris now, and we've been advised that some bad guys are on their way to Bregenz. I've called Helga Kohler, and she'll be in touch with you, she wants to come over to your place for a few days . . . I hope that's O.K.?"

"Of course that's fine Jake . . . What's going on . . . are we in any danger?"

"God Sabrina, I don't think so . . . this is just a cautionary step. We've had some nasty encounters with this guy before, and he is carrying a grudge . . . something he's not going to forget easily. My friend Jacques Manet from Interpol is contacting his office and they will alert the Police in Bregenz and Voralberg area."

"When will you be back?" she asked.

I should arrive this evening . . . I'm taking the train to Zurich, then I'll drive to Bregenz."

"Why don't you stop at my place Jake . . . Helga will be here, so there's no point in going to her place. I'm sure she will want to hear what's going on as much as I do. Sounds exciting!"

"Exciting is not a good way to describe it Sabrina! I don't want to alarm you, but this guy is serious business, and the people he works for are very serious. The man in Paris that we went to see was killed right on the street as we had coffee. The entire meeting ended up to be a disaster!" He did not mean to scare her, but he knew he had to make sure she realized the seriousness of the situation and how deadly Kurt Landau and this whole organization could be.

"Oh my God! I had no idea!" She paused, then carried on, in a very serious voice. "I think Jake, when you arrive, we are going to have a little talk . . . actually a long talk. I don't know if Helga has ever told you what I do . . . I don't mean my work in the tourist office, but what my education and training is. I have a few skills you might be able to use . . . there is more, but we'll have to talk about it later."

As Jake hung up the phone, he thought "Boy, there's more to this girl than what you see, looking forward to another meeting with Sabrina.

CHAPTER 24

Their train ride from Paris back to Zurich was uneventful, the two men fully wrapped in their own thoughts. Once they arrived in Zurich, Jacques checked the schedules for a connecting train to Lyon.

"O.K. Jake, I'll talk to you tomorrow. I've booked a train that heads west through Geneva and will get me into Lyon by tomorrow morning."

Jake said goodbye and went immediately out to get his car from the parking area. Within minutes, he was on the autobahn towards Bregenz. His thoughts were on Sabrina and Helga, but he had to admit, mainly Sabrina. He knew she was safe now, but also knew he could not leave anything to chance. He must be prepared for any eventuality, as he knew Landau was brutally efficient, and now he also had the resources of that Serbian woman and her organization.

He knew nothing of that organization, where it was, how big, what do they do? Correction: he knew what they did! He knew Jacques would have the full resources of Interpol working on those questions, but he also trusted his own crew, and knew they might be just as effective. He asked his smart phone to dial his office as he sped down the highway. The connection was made almost immediately.

"Jake," answered Shannon "Where the hell have you been? Don't you ever check your calls?" She went on for several scathing minutes, obvious worry in her voice.

"Sorry Shannon, I had it turned off during our meeting." Jake offered as an apology.

Shannon came right back, "I see you got that message from Landau! What's going on with him Jake, we're all worried here."

Jake answered, thoroughly chastised, "Oh God, I'm sorry guys . . . it's been a very weird day, and a little upsetting." He proceeded to explain their meeting with Marcel Bergeron, and how he was killed in front of them.

"Oh my God . . ."

Jake continued "And then I got that message from Landau . . . Jacques and I are afraid that he might try to get to us by attacking friends or family. That's why I'm heading back to Bregenz now . . . to be close to Helga and Sabrina."

"Who's Sabrina?" was the obvious question, echoed by three voices.

"Just a friend . . . I'll explain later. The main thing is we have to learn more about our enemy, about the organization that Landau has teamed up with." He then explained what they had learned from Bergeron, about the Serbian woman, Dr. Babić, and her organization Sekhmet Consulting. Alan, you might find something about her in your chemical connections . . . apparently she's an expert in poisons, especially plant based poisons. Peter, see what you can find out about the company, how big it is, where it is based, etc., I'm sure it's somewhere in Serbia, probably Beograd."

A few questions came his way, then he continued. "Jacques Manet will have all of Interpol on this. They've been looking for Landau since last year, so to have it narrowed down to Bregenz, they'll have every police department in the country alerted. They want him almost as much as we do."

"And Jake, don't forget to call Bert Jackson at the F.B.I. . . . he's been trying to get you . . . called several times."

"Oh yeah, I completely forgot him, with this Paris fiasco . . . but he'll be interested in that no doubt!"

After everyone had been brought up to speed, Jake turned his concentration back to his driving. He was almost at Bregenz, he could see the Bodensee off to his left, and started crossing the Rhine as it came down from the Alps. He turned off when his G.P.S. directed him towards the Wagner residence. He could feel some excitement in anticipation of seeing Sabrina again. He called her number to check if everything was O.K. "Yes, Jake, we've been waiting for you. Helga is here, we all want to hear about your mini-vacation in Paris!" Jake could hear laughter in the background.

"You won't laugh when I tell you about my trip." he said. "I'm right outside your place, so I hope you have a drink ready for me!"

It was almost a joyous reunion, dampened only by their knowledge of Jake's experience. As he retold the grim story of their day in Paris, he watched their faces turn from happiness to horror . . . then to fear as he recounted his call from Kurt Landau. Helga was familiar with the story of Landau's crimes, so did not seem particularly shocked.

She mentioned during the discussion "I've told most of this to Sabrina, especially considering her background in this business."

"What background? asked Jake, "I thought she worked in a tourist office."

It was Sabrina's turn to explain. "Yes, I do Jake . . . but my training and education is in criminology, specifically Cyber Crime."

"Oh," said Jake quietly. "I guess I really don't know you . . ."

"Well, Jake, we were getting to that, don't you think? We've only met a couple of times, really haven't had much time to talk. That's why I wanted to talk to you more this time."

"O.K., I guess that's fair." Jake said, a little subdued. "What else can you tell me?" getting a little angry with himself for not knowing more about this beautiful woman.

"First . . . Helga knows all this . . . she's known my family for years. Both my parents are Swiss, and that's where I grew up. When I was at university in Zurich, I specialized in computers, was really good at it, so after I graduated, I joined the F.I.S. in Switzerland."

"I've heard of them when I was in the foreign service." added Jake.

"Yes, you would. The F.I.S., or Federal Intelligence Service is involved with anti-terrorism, extremism and espionage and many other things like cyber attacks and related crimes.

My father was in the F.I.S. for years, which helped me to join. I stayed with them for several years . . . until my father died."

Helga interrupted at this point. "Sabrina's father was killed by a terrorist in an undercover operation."

"Oh, I'm so sorry . . ." Jake offered.

"No, it's O.K., it was some time ago now . . . but it did affect me and stay with me for a long time. Eventually, I quit the force . . . active duty at least . . . which brings me to what I really wanted to tell you. Although I'm working in the tourist office 'officially', I also stay closely connected to the F.I.S. Cyber Crime division . . . and Europol . . . as sort of a consultant. My expertise is in computers, detection and neutralization of Cyber attackers . . . which might . . . or might not . . . help us track down this Landau character."

Jake was speechless. "I had no idea . . ."

"Of course you didn't . . . we just met! She almost yelled at him, obviously upset as well. "Oh Jake, I so wanted to make an impression on you . . . and here I've upset you."

"No . . . no, not at all," he stammered. "You have definitely made an impression on me . . . and this . . . this even more so. Oh Sabrina, if you only knew . . . I don't want to put you in danger, or God forbid . . . lose you!"

"Oh don't worry about that Jake." Helga interrupted. "Sabrina and I have been plotting together while you were enjoying your ride back from Paris."

"Plotting . . . what are you two up to?"

"Sabrina downloaded the latest photos of Landau from the Interpol website, so we are quite familiar with this guy." Before Jake could object, she continued "And in case you didn't notice, this house has a pretty good security system . . . we were tracking you long before you reached the door." She added for emphasis "And besides, we're both armed . . . so just let him try something!"

"Armed . . .? My God Helga, do you have any idea what this guy is capable of?"

"Oh Jake . . . I know you have some history with him," answered Sabrina, "But we're not complete innocents . . . Helga has top marks at her shooting club, and I'm Swiss . . . we are raised with guns in every house. I still have my Glock 17, 9mm Parabellum, and my little favourite, my Baretta Pico, she's a little beauty! That's the one I can carry around. And just so you know . . . nobody in my class could beat me on the range."

It was one more thing to surprise Jake. "Girls . . . I know you have heard about our 'shoot-out' in Bavaria, but that might not be the way he comes at us. We know that he's been using clever and deadly poisons for his last few victims, thanks to his recent association with this Serbian bitch who is some kind of an expert in that field." Jake stopped a moment, thinking. "And, if I know Landau, he will make sure he has some special revenge planned for us . . . at least for me. It scares me because I don't know what he is capable of. So . . . bottom line . . . we have no idea what Herr Landau will do next, and I don't want to leave that up to chance . . . we have to be a little smarter, not just well armed."

CHAPTER 25

As the evening wore on, Jake and the two women established a very solid relationship, based on a combination of shared experiences, apprehension, fear, and love. Jake could scarcely believe what the two had talked about and considered for their defence. Then he remembered they were old friends and had known each other for years.

"Sabrina," asked Jake, "You mentioned your father is dead, where is your mother?"

"Oh I'm sorry Jake, you haven't met her yet . . . her name is Anna, and she's going to love you!" she said with a big smile, blushing profusely. "Oh yes, she's in Switzerland right now, visiting friends. She'll be away for another week or two. Helga is sleeping in her room, and we've made up the guest room for you."

"Oh yes, thank you." answered Jake, secretly wishing he could stay in Sabrina's room. "Helga . . . before I forget, do you remember that little parcel I left with you for safe-keeping last summer?"

"Your gun? Yes Jake, it's at my place, safe and sound." She smiled and then said "I thought you just told us that our guns might not help?"

Jake laughed . . . "Yes, Helga, I did say that. I just thought I'd feel better if I knew where it was . . . just in case . . ." Thinking about the Sig Sauer P-226 semi-automatic brought back some brutal memories, the night he was given the gun by his host on the river barge while they were being attacked by mercenaries. Strangely, the gun also triggered a sense of comfort and safety, a feeling he would have with Landau in his sights.

"I'm sorry ladies, but I must turn in . . . if you point me in the right direction to the guest room. It's been a brutal day, and I have to make some calls first thing in the morning." Jake rose, took his cane and limped out of the room, his leg bothering him more from such a hard day.

The next morning, Jake called Bert Jackson at the F.B.I. in Washington. Bert took his call right away. "Jake, thanks for calling . . . I've been trying to get you . . . but I guess you know that already. Shannon said you were in Paris, and things were not good. Can you expand on that?"

"Yes, I guess that's a pretty good summary of the day 'things were not good', God Bert, you have no idea!" Jake then proceeded to explain about his day in Paris, with emphasis on what Marcel Bergeron had told them just before he was killed. "So you see Bert, I was right . . . someone is eliminating scientists . . . and we don't know why! We now know who, or at least partially who, but we have no idea why they are doing this. You might get some more information from Jacques Manet at Interpol, I think his guys have already got a head start, and they are closer to the problem. It might help if you could check in the states, see if there are any similar deaths . . . deaths that look natural, but are not! I don't know how you can look for things like that, but my guys back at the Vancouver office have figured out a way . . . maybe you could call them."

Bert interrupted, "My God Jake, what kind of can of worms have you opened up now?

"That's not the half of it Bert, in the middle of all this, I got a call from Kurt Landau, threatening me, my friends, my family. Another can of worms, one you are familiar with, eh Bert?"

Jake could feel this tall, African American law enforcement agent cringe at Jake's news. Bert Jackson was an experienced Special Agent, who had distinguished himself in more ways than one. Jake knew that if anyone could help catch Landau, Jackson would be the one.

They talked for a short time, until Bert was interrupted by another call. "I'm sorry Jake, I must take this one, call me if anything else develops."

Jake spent the next hour catching up on calls, to his office, then to Scott Anderson, the WBC reporter. Scott's office answered "I'm sorry Mr. Prescott, but he is on his honeymoon in Europe. Jake suddenly remembered, Scott had planned another trip to Europe for their honeymoon, but his wedding wasn't planned for at least another month. He was probably in Europe now.

He called his office right away. "Shannon . . . do you have Scott Anderson's cell number? All I can get out of his office is that he is in Europe on his honeymoon."

"Well Jake, you came to the right place. I was just talking with Scott . . . yes, he's in Europe, in southern Germany, having a ball, not far from Austria. I told him where you are, so he'll most likely be there within hours. I'll text you his number . . . there!. . . it's already in your phone."

"Thanks Shannon, good news. We just have to make sure he doesn't bump into Landau as he's wandering around Europe. I'll give him a call.

Scott was very excited to receive Jake's call. Especially when Jake started to explain the latest developments. "My God, Jake. It's exactly as you said what might be happening." He paused, then said, even louder "I can't believe that Landau is still on the loose!"

"Well," said Jake, "Interpol have been looking for him for the last year. Now Landau is looking for me!"

Scott's investigative reporter side took over. "My God, what a story, and to think it's still going on. That thing in Paris Jake, you two could have been the victims, not just the whistle blower."

"Yes, I've thought about that . . . there was something in the coffee . . . we don't know what yet, the TOX analysis will take some time."

"How about the woman who did it?"

"I got a call from Jacques at Interpol this morning. The Paris Sûreté know who she is, and they've already talked to her. She said she doesn't know anything about it . . . says she wasn't even in that part of town that morning. So o o o, she's either lying, or someone else was taking her place or impersonating her."

"So that's a dead end . . . so to speak!" Scott said, laughing.

Jake said "Either way Scott, you should get an interesting story out of this. By the way, how's Linda?" referring to his gorgeous fiancé, the co-owner of Seymour Labs in Los Angeles. Linda ran their business with her brother Ed, and were instrumental in solving some key questions in the 'gas attack' case of the previous year.

"Linda's fine, enjoying Europe again. We should be in Bregenz this evening, can we get together for a drink?"

"We can do more than that Scott, I'll treat you two to a delicious Austrian dinner. Try to get a room either in the Bodensee Hotel, or the Weisses Kreuz, that's the White Cross, they're both lovely, and the restaurant we're going to is part of the Weisses Kreuz. Give me call when you're settled, and we'll meet you there for dinner. Tchuss!"

CHAPTER 26

Jake took both ladies out for dinner that evening, as neither of them had met Scott or Linda. "Helga, could we stop by your place on the way . . . you have something there I'd like to pick up."

Helga did not argue . . . she knew Jake wanted to get his gun from her place, he obviously is worried more that he lets on. Jake said to her "I know Helga, that this is against the rules, and I could probably get arrested for it, but I can't help it . . . it just gives me a little extra comfort, considering who might be in the neighbourhood, knowing we have some protection."

When they continued to the restaurant, Jake had a barely visible lump under his jacket, caused by the leather holster with the Sig Sauer P-226 pistol neatly tucked under his left arm.

Scott had managed to get a room at the Weisses Kreuz, so they all met there and after introductions, walked over to the restaurant. The "Gasthaus Goldener Hirschen", or Golden Stag was a classic Austrian restaurant with high beam ceilings and a wonderful varied menu.

It was a warm evening and they all sat out in the enclosed courtyard. Both Scott and Linda were mesmerized by both the decor and the variety of locals who appeared for an evening of fine dining. Rather than some Austrian wine, Jake felt a celebration was in order, so he called for a couple of bottles of Prosecco for them to toast the almost married couple.

Scott started laughing when he looked at the menu. "You'll have to translate some of this for me Jake, I've been depending on Linda to look everything up in her little phrase book/menu translator. I saw the term '*Speisecarte*' yesterday and I thought it meant a list of the spices used. Linda corrected me later . . . it just means 'menu'."

"No problem Scott . . . we have a couple of the local girls here tonight . . . I'm sure they can clarify any of the fine points. This place has some pretty good food, they've been in business for a long time. You'll be able to try some interesting Austrian or German specialties here."

Jake was pleased that they all seemed very comfortable and opened up with the conversation. Linda and Sabrina appeared to be having a good time, giggling and laughing at some private jokes. At one point in their conversation, they were interrupted by a little tinkling sound. Sabrina laughed and grabbed her locket around her neck, a little embarrassed. They all watched her, wondering what was going on. "It's a reminder alarm I set and forgot to cancel."

Puzzled looks returned from the group.

"It's my new phone . . . or actually my smart phone pendant. This amazing little gadget does almost everything my phone does, so if I forget my phone at home, I always have this for important stuff." Everyone wanted to see it and learn more about it. Jake felt a little feeble as he was still trying to figure out his smart phone . . . shrinking it down to the size of a small locket was the next challenge . . . maybe he would eventually get one in a tie-clip! They all laughed when they heard about Jake's potential concerns.

They almost got to the dessert before the subject of criminal activity crept into the conversation. At the insistence of the others, Jake ordered a third bottle of Prosecco, then repeated most of his adventures in Paris, mainly for Linda's benefit, horrifying them both. The first thing Linda said was "Scott darling . . . are we going to be in danger?"

"No, of course not. . . I went through that thing last year . . . missed out on all the good stuff . . . I mean dangerous stuff" he corrected. Linda looked over to Jake, a pleading look on her face. "Jake, please . . . tell me you guys aren't going to repeat what you did last year with this Landau character." She turned to Sabrina, obviously thinking she had some influence on Jake. "Sabrina . . . are you going to let Jake run around the country like before . . . shooting people and getting shot himself?"

Sabrina picked up on the conversation instantly. "No . . . he's definitely not going to do that. We've just been talking about it at home." She glanced at Jake, a serious look of concern on her face. "Jake and I have just met, and I like what I see, so I don't want to lose him already!"

It was Jake's turn to blush, his feelings for Sabrina becoming very obvious. Helga saved them both by jumping in at this point. "Right, we've decided . . . Sabrina and I . . . that we're not going to let Jake out on his own. He has to be with what is called 'a responsible adult'" she laughed. "Seriously, someone like Jacques Manet or now that Scott is here, maybe him. Jake has all kinds of friends that would like to keep him out of trouble."

They continued to have a lovely evening, but never did establish a plan to keep Jake out of trouble . . . he seemed to attract it! And Jake couldn't keep from looking around constantly, checking out everyone that entered the restaurant, or walked by on the street, just in case Landau had already made it to Bregenz.

Kurt Landau had in fact already arrived in Bregenz, and at that moment was watching the dinner party from a safe distance. He had checked into a little pension on the outskirts of town, and later had enjoyed dinner at a local stube. His head kept snapping back and forth with his nervous twitch, as if he were constantly looking for someone. Knowing something about Prescott, he knew that he would be staying with friends, most likely the sister of the scientist he just dealt with in Vancouver. He would just bide his time, he wanted to think this through completely, and not leave anything to chance. As much as he wanted to dispose of that Canadian as quickly as possible, he knew he must go slowly, consider every move. He had already checked a directory of scientists who worked at the environmental centre, and found out where Heinrich lived. After dinner, he slowly drove past the house, only to discover it in total darkness. Rather than do anything rash tonight, he decided to wait until the next day, or possibly the next evening. It was not difficult to figure out where they would be having dinner that evening. He selected the obvious choices of restaurants frequented by tourists wanting a good Austrian meal, one that Prescott would like to show off to his friends. It made things much easier when he discovered them all dining on the outdoor patio. He only had to careful not to be spotted himself.

After watching them for a short time, it was obvious that Prescott was enamoured with one the of the ladies at he table. It was then that an idea started to form in his mind, an idea that might solve all his problems and wishes for revenge.

He wished now that he had more of the special poison he used in Vancouver. He had been warned by Dejana to be careful with it. Although it usually was fatal when injected, just an extremely small amount of her 'new and improved' version could be fatal on contact with the skin. He might find a good chance to use it again here.

As they all walked home to Sabrina's place, Jake couldn't help feel a little nervous as they were out in the open, exposed to a possible attack. He jumped involuntarily when his phone went off in his pocket. He quickly answered it and was pleased to hear Jacques Manet's voice. "Jacques? What's up . . . it's pretty late in Lyon as well, we're just walking home from dinner."

"Yes Jake, I wanted to call as soon as possible . . . we finally got a track on Landau."

"How? Where is he? He said he was coming here . . . we've been watching for him."

"He was using the name 'Frank Kirby', an American businessman. We've been watching all the people who left Vancouver after Heinrich was killed, slowly eliminating them as suspects. This guy first appeared on our screen on a flight from Vancouver to Zurich. He then disappeared again, but we found him with our facial recognition stuff when he flew out of Zurich into St. Petersburg, this time as a German businessman called Ernst Gruber. Once we recognized him and got a name, when then tracked him back to Frankfurt two days after that Russian scientist Boris Klebinov was done in."

"Jesus!" yelled Jake, scaring his dinner companions. "So where is he now?" fearing the answer.

"Well, we don't really know exactly where he's staying, but he did rent a car in Frankfurt, and the last GPS readout we rec'd was in Bregenz!" He paused a moment, then added "So we must assume he's there Jake, in Bregenz, so you have a choice . . . be extremely careful . . . or as the Americans say 'it's time to get out of Dodge!'"

"Jacques . . . don't tell me that's my only options. Have you contacted the local police? that's what Interpol is supposed to do isn't it?"

"Yes Jake . . that's already been done. The police are trying to find where he is staying as we speak. But remember Jake, this guy is very clever, and a master of disguise. We have no idea what his name is or what he looks like now."

Jake thought about that. "You're right . . . so the local police won't have much success finding him." After thanking Jacques and hanging up, they continued walking home as Jake explained what the Interpol agent had just told him. Jake realized it was time to have another meeting to discuss their options.

CHAPTER 27

Little was said for the rest of the evening, each person wrapped in their own thoughts. At breakfast the next morning a call came through from Shannon in Vancouver.

"God, Shannon! What time is it there? Have you been up all night?" Jake asked as he looked at his watch.

"Almost Jake. It's almost six here, I got a call from Jacques Manet last night and I wanted to catch you and raise the boys to fill in the blanks."

"The blanks . . . what do you mean Shannon?"

"Jacques had just talked with you to advise you of Landau's location. He also called us to talk to Alan and Peter about the 'Serbian bitch', Doctor Dejana Babić."

"O.K.," Jake answered, wondering what was next. "Maybe I should talk with Alan and Peter."

"Good . . . here they are."

Jake waited as he heard papers shuffling, coffee cups rattling, and the two men making themselves comfortable. "Jake . . . can you hear . . . we're putting you on speaker-phone."

"That's fine Alan, I can hear you very well. So what did our friend Jacques learn?"

Peter jumped in. "It's not just what he told us, but what we've learned as well."

"I'm waiting guys, can you tell me something?" Jake started to get impatient.

"O.K." answered Alan. "here it is in a nutshell. Our deadly dame, aka Serbian Bitch, aka Dejana Babić, is indeed Serbian, raised by her parents in the Povlen hills near Beograd. Her parents and younger brother were all brutally slaughtered by persons unknown when Dejana was a young woman. It is suspected . . . but not proven . . . that Dejana knew who did this, and within a few years, allegedly wreaked out a brutal revenge on these guys . . . workers from a local exploration company." He paused, shuffling more papers as he looked up something. "Although very little was reported officially, one of the guys dropped dead of a heart attack while he was enjoying a drink in a bar where Dejana worked. Sound familiar?"

Jake interrupted "You said 'allegedly' . . . is this just speculation, or does Jacques have any actual proof of all this?"

"Well, that's the problem, none of this has actually been proven in a court of law, it's just what various investigators have assembled over the years. Apparently Jacques has a sizable file on this lady."

"Wow . . . if most of her history is true, no wonder she has a thing about revenge and methods thereof."

"And . . . about the other guys that crossed her, not a great deal is known but I managed to find a note that within a year of the first guy, a couple more guys from the company died from a severe stomach ailment. It was passed off as a food poisoning thing, but nobody else got it. No doubt about it, she's good at what she does . . . she had good training. Her father was a local school teacher, and her mother was an expert on local plants and herbs. This is where she picked up some important information about poisonous plants and what they can do to you. She attended university in Beograd and got her degree in Botany, specializing in organic chemistry."

Peter jumped in at this point. "Her company   such as it is . . . is based in a small laboratory facility in the woods of the Povlen hills . . . probably where she grew up. She is quite successful at her art, and her fees are substantial . . . if her bank accounts are correct."

"Her bank accounts . . .?" Jake started.

"Don't ask . . . that's information you don't need to know" Peter added.

Alan wasn't finished. "Like I said, this gal is very good at what she does. We managed to analyze the bits of poison that was left on Heinrich's water bottle. It was almost as we suspected, a form of Batrachotoxin, but a little different. The only way I have heard about how you get it is to piss off some special frogs, and collect the poison from little glands on their back. It's how the natives poison their darts for hunting. I guess that's why they're referred to as 'poison dart frogs'. Apparently they hold the frogs over the fire, that really gets them agitated . . . an interesting fact . . . if these frogs are raised in captivity, they do not have this poison secretion. She's obviously developed a method of producing the poison, because it's quite rare in nature. Not only that, this woman has managed to modify the chemistry a little, just enough to make it transportable and extremely deadly. I'm sure they will find that the poison used in Paris will a little different from the norm. That one was probably a variation of digitalis from foxgloves, or possibly a Maitotoxin, which also works very fast."

"There is, however, a little problem. Jacques explained it to us. Despite all this information, it makes for interesting reading, but it is entirely circumstantial . . . they cannot charge her with anything and have enough real evidence to prove it."

Silence then surrounded them.

"Is that all?' asked Jake.

"Is that all . . .? yelled Alan, "What the hell did you expect?"

"No Alan, that's not what I meant." pleaded Jake. "You guys have done a fantastic job. No wonder we've been wandering around in a fog."

Silence filled the air once again, until Shannon jumped in. "What? Is that it? What are you going to do now . . . track down this woman and shoot her or something?"

"No Shannon . . ." Jake pleaded. What we do now is leave it up to the police, to Jacques and all of his cohorts. It's up to them to gather enough evidence to justify arresting her and stopping this horror."

"Yes," answered Shannon . . . "I know how that goes . . . as you do too Jake. The wheels of justice will slowly grind, while she carries on killing people. This is what happened last year, until you guys got pissed off and went after the bad guys. I sort of feel sorry for this woman . . . just think about what she's been through . . . you can hardly blame her. If it wasn't for those guys killing her parents, she might have become a world famous chemist or pharmaceutical genius. God knows she has the smarts to do it!"

Jake answered very quietly. "I know what you're saying Shannon, but we can't turn the clock back at this stage. She has set things in motion . . . we can't stand back and let things go. We have to try to counter some of her moves, either slow her down or stop her." In a way, Jake hated himself for saying it, as he knew exactly how Shannon felt, how he himself felt, his frustration with the slow grinding of the system. It had got him into trouble several times before, and he hoped it would not repeat itself with this problem.

"Thanks Shannon, and thanks to you two guys . . . you've done a fantastic job. I would ask one more favour . . . pass this on to Jacques . . . the stuff he doesn't know, and all of it to Bert Jackson of the FBI. I'll try to fill in Scott Anderson, as he is right here in Bregenz." He paused, then added "I'm not sure if Jacques already told you this, but Landau is here in Bregenz as well. Jacques has the local police looking for him, but we're going to be extra cautious as well." All he could hear from the phone was a collective groan.

An early morning fog had almost disappeared as Jake and Sabrina went for a walk down by the Lake. The sun was already high enough they could feel its warmth, and enjoy the bright colours of the trees and foliage around them. Jake felt a little embarrassed as he struggled along with his cane, trying vainly to keep up with her. He was excited to finally get Sabrina by herself, and he took advantage of the situation to try to express his feelings toward her. He failed miserably. She listened to Jake at first with a sense of amusement, which quickly turned serious as she realized that he was stumbling over the simplest expressions of love, something she was just learning about this gentle man. To help him along, she stopped walking, then turning to him and taking his face in her hands, she gave him a soft, warm kiss. "You don't have to get so emotional Jake, I'm pretty sure I know how you feel . . I feel the same way."

Jake responded in kind, clutching her fiercely and returning the kiss. He body started to respond in other ways and he decided they had to cool things down. "Oh Sabrina . . . I feel so guilty in some ways . . . I thought that Christa was the love of my life . . . I was devastated when she was killed."

"Of course you were Jake . . . that whole event was heartbreaking. I know it's rough, and I feel a little selfish when I say that she's gone . . . I'm here, so let's try to move on."

Jake realized she was right, they had something very special developing here, and he couldn't lose the chance for happiness.

She laughed, being careful not to tease him too much. "Besides, I have to go to work today, but I'm sure we can continue this conversation later today."

Jake caught the look on her face and smiled, "I'm sure we can" he agreed.

By the time they had finished their walk, both of them felt very good about their progress and their future prospects. It must have shown on their faces, considering the comments they received when they entered the house.

CHAPTER 28

K urt Landau was frustrated. He knew Prescott was in Bregenz, but did not know where he was staying. He hesitated and did not follow them home from the restaurant the evening before, as it was almost certain he would be spotted. He also did not know who the lady was that Prescott was so involved with, but he had seen her briefly in the tourist office earlier. He made sure it was the first thing he managed to do the next morning. Driving over to the tourist office early, he watched until Sabrina showed up for work. He was right . . . it was the same girl. He was very careful and did not want to approach the girl alone, so he waited patiently until another employee had arrived and a couple of tourists entered to ask for information. With his impromptu disguise of sunglasses and a baseball cap, he entered the little space, browsing through some of the racks of brochures. When he had the opportunity, he talked with the second girl about some of the local sights, staying immersed in a map to make it harder to see his features. He dare not ask about the other girl, in case he might raise a suspicion, but he did see her name tag pinned on that lovely breast. "Sabrina" . . . He filed that away in his memory, knowing he would need that information to complete the details in his developing 'Jake Prescott' plan.

This was a situation which Dejana called 'a fool's errand'. He knew that to follow his ideas of getting even with Jake through his new girl-friend was a little risky, one which could back-fire on him. He stopped thinking about it and returned to the task at hand. His employer had another job for him, one he was looking forward to. After checking out of his pension, he stopped by the train station to check connections to Lyon, France.

He ended up driving to Zurich and unknowingly booked the same connections as Jacques Manet had done several days before. If Landau had known this, it would have increased his frustration even more, as his new assignment was the elimination of M. Jacques Manet.

Dejana was also very troubled. She was not only allowing Landau to violate one of her most important rules, but now she herself was doing the same. For years, she had managed to keep her personal biases out of her business. After satisfying her early urges of revenge years before, she soon realized how dangerous that could be, as there were too many loose ends that could be traced back to her. So, by cutting all ties to anything personal, she had managed to survive in total obscurity, no connections to her, every project was anonymous, protected by a cloud of confusion.

But recently, this group of scientists and other investigators led by Prescott and Manet, had picked up enough clues to deduce what was happening. This made it very difficult for her to stay anonymous. For this reason, she had wavered from her hard and fast rules to let Landau stalk Prescott, to try to eliminate him from the picture. Stupidly, he had warned Prescott, putting him on guard, and driving him underground. One more reason not to let personal vendettas enter the game. Landau was trying to place his feelings ahead of the job, and to try to threaten Prescott with the mistaken belief he would feel threatened and try something stupid. Instead, he was a lot more clever than estimated, and disappeared. After what Dejana had learned recently about Jake Prescott, she realized he was very smart, knew the language, knew the territory well, and had lots of friends and colleagues he could call on. All things that Landau did not seem to understand.

For these reasons, she changed Landau's assignment to the other thorn in her side, Jacques Manet, that bothersome Interpol Englishman with a French name that kept popping up like a bad penny with more clues to follow. "Why doesn't he stay in his office like he is supposed to?" she asked herself. She was very aware of Interpol's mandate, as well as their legal limitations. She also knew not to under-estimate their skills and their capabilities. This Manet was just one of many skilled agents from 194 countries, all very skilled in crime fighting. She was particularly concerned with Interpol's secure communication system, the I-24/7. This provided member countries access to a huge criminal database, 24/7. This system made it very uncomfortable, even impossible for criminals to travel internationally, or get away with anything. Fortunately, she had her own contacts within the police system, contacts that kept her abreast of the latest I-24/7 notices that were active. She knew that this was the way the authorities had tracked Landau out of Vancouver and beyond. She knew she had to limit his future travel to priority locations only.

Interpol's international network and I-24/7 system was in action at the same time Dejana was thinking about it. As Landau left Zurich on the train for Lyon, the facial recognition system was providing real time data to a computer database in Lyon. Certain features were recognized and flags went up to notify the authorities involved with the case. Because of the 24/7 operation of the system, A notice was on Jacques Manet's desk before Landau reached the halfway mark on his journey.

Jacques was a little surprised, knowing that Landau had been in Bregenz, most likely looking for Jake. As he thought about Landau's move some more, he suddenly realized another possibility . . . Landau was coming for him! He wasted no time, punching his intercom, "Annette, would you please call building security? Have somebody come up to see me . . . I might have a job for them. And connect me to Lyon secûrité.

Once he was connected to his contact in the local police office, he explained about the possibility of Landau arriving on a train from Zurich within a couple of hours. It did not take long to convince him to take immediate action. They would make sure M. Landau would have an appropriate welcome. He then picked up his phone and called Jake Prescott.

M. Landau, however was even more clever than Jacques had calculated. He had been watching the station activity at each stop along the way . . . watching for anything out of the ordinary. As they reached Lausanne, his suspicious nature and trained eye spotted a couple of plain-clothes agents wandering the platform, obviously not interested in the train, just who was getting off. Bells went off in Kurt's head . . . who are they searching for? Knowing a few details about Interpol's tracking and warning system, he had to assume something had triggered the system about his travels. He texted Dejana and asked her to confirm . . . knowing she had some inside information. Within minutes, she had confirmed that they had in fact tracked him and were most likely waiting for him in Lyon. He wasted no time, as soon as the train started up again, he prepared to get off at the nearest stop. It was almost a day later by the time he got back to Zurich, so he checked into a hotel to rest and decide what his next step was.

Jacques Manet was not surprised when his phone rang to advise him that Landau was not on the train. He knew Landau was clever, but this reeked of insider information. How did he know they were waiting for him? "Annette, call that guy in security again . . . I want a meeting *tout suite*! Somebody is leaking information here. And call Lyon secûrité as well, I want to talk to the guy they had running this thing!"

By the time they figured out what might have happened, or what Landau might have done, he was long gone, and they were sitting there with their high-tech system sucking wind . . . beaten by someone thinking one step ahead of them.

CHAPTER 29

Kurt Landau was rested and refreshed by the time he returned to Bregenz. After his near disaster on his trip to Lyon, he had decided to continue his Bregenz activities because he knew Jake was still here, and even more important now . . . Sabrina was here! Sabrina . . .Sabrina . . . the name rolled around in his mouth until he could taste the revenge . . . bitter-sweet revenge. He could hardly wait to get started, but he knew he had to be careful . . . one mistake and he would be in trouble. He knew she worked in the little tourist information office, but he did not know if she was part-time, or a full-time employee. He realized he needed to learn more . . . and he also realized he had no idea what he was going to do! Kidnap her? . . . How? . . . and then what? This kind of thing was definitely not high on his list of skill-sets. He could drug her . . . how? He did have some drugs that would do the job, but how would he accomplish that? He did not want to kill her . . . yet . . . he would lose his only bargaining chip with Prescott. He decided he would just bide his time until he came up with a plan . . . he could not take a chance of losing this opportunity.

In the meantime, Jake found himself spending more time back at Helga's place. After spending one night at the Wagner's, he realized he could not stay there forever. It was a little too close to Sabrina. She carried on with her life, going to work as usual, returning home, and it was up to Jake to suggest going out or doing something together. Both of them were having a difficult time controlling their emotions, so a very strict regime of controls and time use kept things under control.

Jake took advantage of the extra time to keep in touch with his office and projects at home, and also to learn all he could about Sabrina from Helga, who had known Sabrina and her parents for years.

"She's a lovely girl Jake, and you should be very careful and treat her right."

"Of course I'll 'treat her right' Helga, but what do you mean, 'be very careful'?"

"Well, first, she's a good friend of mine, as well as her mother . . . ever since her father was killed. Sabrina is a very special girl, very strong in many ways, very talented, but also very innocent and naive when it comes to influences and suggestions from others."

"I have seen some of that already, Helga. I wouldn't do anything to hurt her, believe me."

"It's not her I'm worried about Jake, she's learned how to protect herself and has taken steps over the years to reinforce those skills . . . it's you I'm worried about . . . if you step out of line, you could find yourself 'on your ass', so-to-speak. Her training with the FIS really helped build her self confidence, and she keeps honing her self-defence skills all the time."

"Wow! I'll make sure I behave myself," Jake laughed, "but seriously, I'm really pleased to hear that, with these 'bad guys' lurking around, it's nice to know she can look after herself if needed."

One of the 'bad guys', namely Kurt Landau was indeed lurking around. With a more efficient and effective disguise, he was spending a lot of time walking around Bregenz, checking out the tourist office, hoping to see Sabrina or Jake to establish where either of them were living. He couldn't go somewhere and ask about Jake, he didn't even live here, so most people wouldn't know him. He hesitated to ask about Sabrina, as he could not establish a reason that would sound appropriate to one of the locals. He finally went into the tourist office one day, and very casually asked "Is Sabrina not in today? I was talking to her yesterday and she helped me a lot."

"No, I'm sorry sir, Sabrina only works mornings during weekdays . . . can I help you?"

"No, thank you. I just wanted to thank her for her help. I was asking about the Pfänderbahn, and she was a great help."

Kurt felt that almost any tourist might have questions about the Pfänder, a high mountain just behind the city of Bregenz, with a mountain cable car that takes sight-seers up over one thousand meters for a fantastic view of the Bodensee and surrounding the countryside of Austria, Germany and Switzerland. He had picked up a brochure on the ride the day before, but felt it would be natural for visitors to ask additional questions. The exercise had gained him one more little bit of information . . . she works on weekday mornings. Kurt stored that away, a little disappointed as he had hoped to learn more.

Unfortunately for Kurt, his little ruse back-fired and drew more attention to him. When Sabrina went to work the next day, her co-worker commented. "Oh Sabrina, that man you helped with the Pfänder information dropped by to thank you. He was very pleased."

"What man?" vainly trying to remember someone who she helped. "I don't remember . . . what did he say, what did he look like?" Suddenly her defences were on guard . . . she could not remember giving advice to anyone on the Pfänder for some time, certainly not the day before.

"He was fairly tall, and he had really dark eyes and dark eyebrows . . . I remember that about him." She paused, then added "And he was always looking around, as if he was looking out for someone."

Cold chills went up Sabrina's spine . . . Landau! She was certain . . . how did he find her and what does he want? She didn't have to think very long to figure out the answers to those questions.

The other girls noticed the change in her appearance, the colour had drained from her face. "Sabrina . . . what's the matter . . . what is it . . . who is this guy?"

She turned to them and replied "It's a long story . . . I'll have to tell you another time. Right now I have to go home." She pulled out her phone and called Jake. Of course, Jake's voice-mail cut in with a lame excuse that he was busy. Knowing Jake was probably not yet tech-smart enough to figure out his call-waiting feature, she left a message. "Jake . . it's Sabrina. Landau's in town . . . he was at my office asking for me. I'm heading home now, please come as soon as you get this message." A few more gulps of air . . . then "I'm scared Jake . . . I know how dangerous this guy is."

Sabrina felt vulnerable. She always walked to work . . . it wasn't far . . . but now it seemed forever. Halfway home she wished she had called a taxi, or even waited for Jake to pick her up. What was she thinking?

Kurt Landau was not far behind. He was driving his little rental car, trying not to get too close to Sabrina. He realized his questions at the tourist office had triggered a response he had not counted on. Fortunately his constant surveillance had paid off.

She had somehow recognized that it was he that was asking the questions, and was obviously heading home.

"Good!" he mumbled to himself. "Now I'll find out where she lives." Before long, she turned off the street to a modest little cottage surrounded by flower gardens.

Kurt realized he was running out of chances . . . he did not want her to go inside. He pulled up in front, jumping out of the car as Sabrina was struggling at the front door with her keys. He reached her just as she opened the door. He was right behind, pulling something out of his pocket as he pushed her inside. She turned to confront him, ready to do battle, but Kurt was too quick, pulling out a small hypodermic needle and jabbing it into her extended arm. To late, she realized what had happened. As she quickly faded away into oblivion, her only thoughts were for Jake . . . and the life she could have had with him.

CHAPTER 30

It wasn't long after that Jake played back his voice-mail messages. His worst fears realized, he called Sabrina right away, but there was no answer. He called the tourist office and talked to one of the other girls.

"Sorry Mr. Prescott, Sabrina went home." They did not know Jake, so were hesitant to give out any further information. "I can only tell you she was very upset . . . I think something to do with the man who came in asking for her yesterday."

"The man . . . who was that, do you know?"

She described briefly what she had told Sabrina, what had upset her so much.

Jake knew then what had triggered Sabrina's frantic voice-mail message of Landau being there, possibly stalking Sabrina. Why was she not answering her phone? He tried again . . . someone answered the phone. "Hello Mr. Prescott . . . I'm sure you know who this is . . . and that I have your little girl-friend Sabrina."

"Landau you sonofabitch! You'd better not hurt her, or I'll have your balls for book-ends!"

"My . . . that's a quaint expression Jake . . . but you do know how serious this situation is?"

"Let me talk to her Landau . . . put her on the phone!"

"No, I'm sorry, but she is having nap right now . . . I'll have to get back to you." He hung up the phone. Jake couldn't believe it! Even with all the warnings and information on Landau's whereabouts, they still fell into his trap. How could he have been so stupid, so complacent? He should have been guarding her, or at least arranging for extra security to help them.

Helga noticed Jake's distress. "What is it Jake . . . what's happened?"

"He's got Sabrina . . . that goddamn Landau has taken Sabrina. I don't know how he did it, but it should not have happened!" He couldn't believe he had been so stupid! Even with all the warnings and earlier threats, he managed to be be an easy target for this arch enemy.

Helga wasn't having any of it. "Pull yourself together Jake. Don't blame yourself so much, you know you're dealing with an ex master-spy, skilled in the art of deception. Sabrina should have known better than to walk home alone. We agreed to that several nights ago at her place. The main thing now . . . what are you going to do about it?"

Jake had already moved into action. "Helga, you're right . . . could you please call the hotel and try to catch Scott Anderson or Linda. I want to talk to him before they move on. I'm calling Jacques Manet at Interpol . . . I'm sure he'll want to know. Then I have to call my office. I need some tech advice from Peter."

Jacques Manet was not surprised at the news. "Oh God Jake, I'm so sorry. We knew he was there, but we didn't think he would get this bold. Call the local police and give them the information. And . . . for God's sake Jake, don't go off half-cocked and try chasing this guy yourself! You know how that turned out last year?"

Jake wasn't really listening . . . as Jacques talked to him, he was already thinking what he was going to do to Landau when he caught him . . . and he would catch him.

It wasn't until he was talking to his office that he realized just how difficult this might be. He had no idea where they were, where Landau might have taken her, or what he had in mind for her. Several possibilities came to mind, raising his fears and anger even more.

Peter had been listening to Jake's story. "So, Jake, when you called Sabrina, Landau answered . . . so he's got her phone obviously. Do you know what kind of phone she has Jake?"

"I don't know . . . no wait . . . it's a smart phone, I think the same as mine. Why is that important Peter?"

"All these phones have built-in G.P.S. capability, Jake. We might be able to track her phone by that. Give me her number."

Jake gave Peter the number and he disappeared . . . doing his tech thing. It didn't take long and he was back. "Here Jake, here's the coordinates . . . you'll have to check on a map . . . Google says it's right in Bregenz, Austria."

Jake was encouraged. He checked the location further and found it was Sabrina's address. Surely she wasn't still at home?

Peter answered his question. "That's just where her phone is Jake . . . I'm sure if she was taken, her phone would be left behind, this guy is smart enough to know that."

Once again, Jake was disappointed.

Scott phoned as soon as Jake stopped talking with Vancouver. "What the hell Jake . . . haven't they got this guy yet? Linda and I are so sorry, but I'm glad we're here . . . maybe there's something we can do to help. Jesus Jake, I figure I could make a good career by just following you around! In any case, we're still in town, decided to stay a few more days. We went hiking up that mountain behind the town yesterday . . . lovely." He stopped, then added "But enough of what we did . . . what can we do to help?"

"I don't know Scott . . . I suppose just come over and Linda can keep Helga company. She's trying to get ahold of Sabrina's mother in Switzerland . . . I don't know how that's going to go. I'm going over to the tourist office . . . meeting the police there . . .

they want to talk to the girls that saw him. Maybe you could meet me there, it will bring you up to speed. Then I'm going to get back to Jacques, see what he knows about Landau's favourite hiding spots . ., where would he take Sabrina . . . someplace he would feel safe keeping her."

Kurt Landau was indeed heading towards a safe hiding place. After abducting Sabrina, he quickly headed south on route 202, wanting to put as much distance as possible between him and Bregenz. He knew it would not be long before they had his rental car information and they would be looking for him all over the territory. He eventually crossed the Rhine canal, then continued through Höchst into Switzerland. Staying off the main roads, he then crossed the old Rhine, heading east through Rheineck and towards the lake to the little known airport called Flughafen St. Gallen Altenrhein. He had used this airport many times in the past and had a small warehouse close to the field. He checked his watch as he pulled up in front. He quickly went in and opened the large doors, he then drove the car inside and closed the doors. Checking his watch again, he figured he had made good time, and they would be hard pressed to trace his steps.

Sabrina was starting to regain consciousness as he pulled her out of the car and pushed her into a small room at the rear of the warehouse. It was outfitted with another small table, chair and a cot for sleeping. "This is where I used to work overtime when I had shipments coming and going." he explained to Sabrina as she woke up, confused. "There's a small washroom at the back, so there's no need for you to leave this room." At that point, a small jet was taking off from one of the runways outside, shaking the little building with its noise.

"Who are you and what are you doing?" she asked, not letting on she knew exactly who he was. "Why have you done this . . . what do you want from me?"

Landau started to laugh . . ." I don't need anything from you, Miss Sabrina . . . it's your pesky boyfriend who I want . . . Mr. Jake Prescott!"

"Jake . . . but why . . . what has he done to you?"

Landau face turned rigid, his skin turning red, his eyes darker, and his mouth tightening up in a straight line, his cheek bones becoming more prominent. "What has he done to me . . . what hasn't he done to me? That man, along with that idiot Englishman from Interpol ruined my life. I had things all figured out . . . and they interfered, meddled in things that should not have concerned them."

Sabrina knew the other side of the story, but said nothing, not wanting to give away anything that might help this psycho get his way. She started to reach for her phone, just to see if was still there.

"Oh no, missy . . . no phones." He laughed, obviously thinking he was very clever. "I have disposed of your little phone back in Bregenz . . . after I had a little talk with Jake."

"He knows I'm here . . . you talked to him?" She could feel her pendant watch hanging down between her breasts, but safely tucked under her blouse. She said nothing more, a little idea forming in her mind.

"Yes, I talked to him, so he knows. I told him I would call later, once I figure out what we're going to do with you." With that, he left the room and she could hear him locking the door behind him.

Sabrina looked around, inspecting her prison closely. As she entered the building, she saw that it was well built with double walls of corrugated metal for better temperature control in both summer and winter. To complicate things more, the room inside also had double metal walls. This type of construction basically closed her in an effective Faraday cage . . . something her cell phone's signal might not penetrate. No windows, only the one door, no phone outlets or other means of contacting the outside world. She only hoped her little smart watch would do the job. She knew she had to work fast, before he returned. Pulling out her pendant from under her blouse, she tried to establish a signal to send something. There were 'no bars', as the expression goes. Basically no reception at all in that room. "Damn!" she cried to herself. "And I thought I was being so smart . . . why doesn't this damn thing work?" She left the phone turned on, just in case the reception improved. Unfortunately, her spirits were dropping, she had really hoped that Jake would come and rescue her, but it looked less likely that would happen.

CHAPTER 31

Back in Bregenz, Jake was trying to explain to the local police what had happened, and how he, a Canadian, fitted into this picture. They had already received a lot of information from Interpol, specifically from Jacques Manet regarding the situation between Jake and Kurt Landau. Their respective history from the previous year seemed to confuse the officers, adding to their misunderstanding of the situation. Jacques had also complicated things by adding the fact that Sabrina was an ex FSI officer, something they take very seriously. The FIS in Switzerland had been notified and an agent was already on his way from Zurich. Helga had managed to notify Sabrina's mother, and she was also on her way back to Bregenz.

Jake was in a turmoil. He felt frustrated because he had very little control of the situation. He had to admit that things were moving along, almost as fast as he could have wished. He bounced a few ideas off Scott Anderson, just to get his opinion of the situation and to see if he had any ideas. Scott had covered many abductions and kidnappings over the years, and knew a few things more than Jake did about the techniques and actions of both the kidnappers and the police. This was Jake's first kidnapping experience and he was at a loss as to what to expect and what to do.

The police set up a command post in Helga's house, with full time communication links with their counterparts located over in

Sabrina's house. They had found her phone just inside the door, no doubt dumped there when she was abducted.

"I've already had my tech guy in Vancouver try that." Jake offered. "All he came up with is Sabrina's address . . . because her phone was left here."

"That's OK, Mr. Prescott, leave it with us, we have some pretty smart guys working on this."

"Just call me Jake, please."

Jake's phone started to ring. He glanced at the phone and saw that it was Landau! He could hardly stop himself from answering and screaming at his enemy. Signalling the police tech guy, they all went into action. Within seconds, they were ready. Jake answered the phone. "You sonofabitch . . . you'd better not harm that girl. Let me talk to her now!"

"Might I remind you Jake . . . I'm calling the shots here." He paused, most likely trying to prolong Jake's agony . . . but for her sake, I'll let you say Hello."

The frantic voice of Sabrina came on. "Oh Jake . . . I'm so sorry . . ."

"Sabrina . . . are you alright . . . has he hurt you?"

"No, everything is fine here . . . I just keep trying to think good thoughts, remembering good memories . . . you know, like our evening at the restaurant, and the things we discussed. It helps cheer me up."

"Here . . . give me that phone . . . you've talked enough. Well, Jake . . . as you can tell, she's just fine, but I'm afraid we've run out of time. I'll call again."

He disconnected the phone before they had a chance to trace his call. The police were disappointed, but Jake was excited. "She's OK," he kept feeling there was something else happened during their brief conversation. Instead of being frantic and blubbery, she seemed cool and controlled, like she was trying to get his attention, tell him something. "Our evening at the restaurant." she had said . . . "the things we discussed". What had they discussed? The one thing that they all remembered was Sabrina's smart watch. Was she trying to tell him to check for the signal, or was she going to do something that might help. Not taking any chance, he turned to the tech expert and said "Franz . . . please do your tech thing now . . . look for the GPS information . . . Sabrina has one of those smart watches . . . a pendant around her neck. Let's hope Landau doesn't catch on. During our conversation, I think Sabrina is trying to tell us she's going to try something." At that point, one of the specialists came over, looking quite excited about something.

"What is it Franz . . . did you find something?"

"Yes and no sir. We can't communicate with either of the phones, but we do know where they were going from the time she was abducted for about a half hour. It obviously wasn't her phone, because that's still here. So it was probably because of her smart watch she had with her."

"Where?" He turned to another man "Give me that map . . . can you show me where they went?"

"Yes, we thought they might head north up to Germany somewhere, or even across and down to Italy." He pointed to the map and added "No, it appears they headed south, across to Die Schweiz. We have cell phone signals and GPS data right into Die Schweiz, right over to the Rhine canal and possibly the Old Rhine . . . unfortunately, we lose track of her there, something happened, or the phone was turned off."

Jake knew they were referring to Switzerland, called Die Schweiz in that area. That was an area he hadn't thought they would go either.

"So . . . can you track her now . . . have you tried again?" Jake asked, frantic to hear some good news.

"No, but we'll keep trying."

Jake grabbed the map again. "Let me see that." he said, hoping the answer would jump off the paper. "Just how far did you actually get signals . . . do you have a spot where they stopped?"

The officer in charge pointed to an area on the map. "Somewhere around here . . . just past Rheineck."

"So what's in that area? It looks like a semi-industrial area."

"Well, no . . . it's mainly farm land all the way along that highway, until you get close to the village of Altenrhein, out near the airport."

"Airport?" asked Jake, suddenly interested. "What kind of an airport is it?"

"Just a single runway airfield, but they do have small jets come and go . . . a few warehouses here and there. They have a real interesting flight museum out there as well. I took my kids to it last summer."

"Warehouses?" asked Jake.

The officer caught on immediately, yelling for his colleague. "Heinz, do we have any information on the businesses near the airport at Altenrhein?"

"Here, Boss, as soon as you guys started talking about Die Schweiz, I went into another website, and checked with our Swiss counterparts. Most of the buildings on that site are associated with small flight companies or airplane maintenance or supply outfits."

"You said 'most of them'?"

"Yeah, there's a few outlying buildings either owned or rented out to private firms . . . usually people in the shipping business, you know . . . import, export."

Jake stood up. "That's it!" he announced. "That's where they are."

"What makes you think that Jake? Why there?"

"Just think . . . if the watch was not turned off . . . something else killed the signal. What better way than to go into a well built, double walled, metal warehouse. Essentially a Faraday cage!"

That was enough information to trigger some action. Several officers were scrambling around, becoming mobile. "I'll call for some Swiss support . . . we'll need their help as it's on their turf."

CHAPTER 32

Dejana Babić stared at her computer screen, her temper flaring. Normally, she was not bothered by the actions of others, no matter how stupid they appear. But this! That damned Landau had gone off the rails again. Reports coming in from her contacts in certain police departments kept her informed of actions of some of her 'employees'.

First, she had to abort the Interpol business, after Landau was recognized and a welcoming party was ready for him. Then the idiot does another stupid thing in his vendetta with Jake Prescott. He actually kidnapped Prescott's girl friend from her home in Bregenz! That was too much, she had to make other arrangements.

She still put some priority on the Interpol business. There was the biggest threat, the man with the most potent organization behind him. Prescott was a nuisance, but she could wait and deal with him later. She decided to be extra careful, making sure there were no loose ends, no connections back to her. She had always operated that way, the main reason why she had survived and succeeded for so long. She had a reliable contact in Lyon, one she had depended on for some time for information and data she could not access any other way. She decided it was time to test this contact to see how good she really was. After a few text messages and a secure telephone conversation, she had finally put the wheels in motion to eliminate one of the irritations in her life, M. Jacques Manet.

Malina Aleksov had lived in Lyon for several years, spoke French like a native, and had a coveted government job that gave her excellent access to the Interpol offices. Her job as a Serbian/French translator in Interpol provided her access to a lot of confidential information. Over the years, she had managed to glean small but reasonably important bits of information to pass on to Dejana.

This, however, was a different situation. She knew it would provide a good payday . . . but to be responsible for taking a man's life . . . that was another matter. She also knew that her family back in Serbia would benefit as well. She pulled out the small package that Dejana had given her a few months ago. "Just in case I need you to do something" she had said, "Something very important."

Malina inspected the package. Opening it up, she pulled out a small vial of liquid. Dejana insisted that she be very careful of this liquid. "Do not open the vial until you want to use it." She had said emphatically.

Dejana looked at her computer again, hoping to get some further information on Landau's situation. Sure enough, a little text message informed her that the police were tracking Prescott's girlfriend by her cell phone, and they were closing in on Landau. She immediately turned to her phone and punched out a short message.

———⟨w⟩———

Landau was getting impatient . . . he was not used to the waiting game, especially when he had no control over the game. What was he thinking? He now realized it had been a stupid move to kidnap Sabrina. What was he going to do with her? How does this affect Prescott? Every time he thought about that man, his temper would flare.

He went out of the warehouse to pick up some food and water at a local convenience store in the village. He kept aware of his surroundings . . . there were no police lurking around. He carried his bag of groceries back into the warehouse and set them on the little table. He then walked over and unlocked the door to Sabrina's prison. "If you behave yourself, you can join me for some food and water" Sabrina was hungry, but more important, she wanted to learn more about the warehouse and about her captor.

"OK" she agreed. Coming out of her cell, she was glad that he hadn't shackled her or tied her up. She played the innocent victim so he did not feel threatened in any way. She sat down at the table and watched Landau hand out their rations for the day.

"Why have you done this . . . what are you going to do to me?" She asked. "You must know this will not end well for you."

"What do you know, little missy? There is more to this story than you might think."

Sabrina was tempted to tell him just how much she knew, but again withheld her comments.

She stared around, trying to find a week spot in the building's siding and insulation . . . a spot where her phone might work.

Suddenly, the silence was interrupted by a soft tinkling sound. Landau's head spun around, looking to see where the sound came from, just in time to see Sabrina trying to cover her breasts to smother the sound. He took two steps towards her and pulled her arms back. Realizing what she was trying to cover, he slapped her violently across the face. "*Scheisse*!" he screamed, "you little bitch!" He grabbed the pendant's chain and ripped it from her neck. Quickly looking at the pendant, he realized what it was. "What have you done . . . have you actually sent out a message?"

"Yes, Herr Landau, and they now know where we are. Jake should be here any minute to kick your ass!"

"Wha . . . you know who I am?" He looked at her with a different expression now. "Oh . . . little miss Sabrina, I underestimated you. You're a lot more clever than I thought."

"You have no idea . . ." she answered, a defiant look on her face.

He pulled out a gun, pointing it towards Sabrina. I should blow you away right now!" he said very slowly. "Get back in your room . . . now!"

Sabrina did not argue. "If possible, pick the times and location for your battles" had been her advice in training. She couldn't remember if it was from her trainer, or from the Art of War by Sun Tzu. She calmly walked back to the little room, and went over to sit down. Landau was in such a state, he could hardly control his temper. At that point, his phone pinged a little signal. He quickly looked down, his features darkening as he read the message. It was from Dejana: "The police know where you are! They are on their way."

"Scheisse! That little bitch!" Even though he would like to kill her at this point, he knew he might need her later, maybe a bargaining chip.

"Come along missy" he said as he opened her door again. "We're leaving . . . I've just had word that your boyfriend is on his way with the police. This is all your fault!" he was almost pathetic, Sabrina thought. But she knew he was still very dangerous and might try some desperate moves . . . she had to be ready.

They moved out towards the parked car. Neither of them had anything to carry, so Landau's full attention was on his pistol, ominously pointed directly at Sabrina, and his cell phone in the other hand. "Get in" he said, pointing to the car. She knew she did not want to get into the car. Doing that severely limited her options for escape, which she knew she must try.

"Too late, Landau! I hear them pulling up outside now . . ." she said, hoping to change his direction of attention.

It worked, at least partially. As he glanced towards the large door, she grabbed at his arm holding the gun. He spun to counter the grip and swung at her with his other hand. She dropped, spinning around, landing a back kick in his stomach, knocking the gun away. He was furious, swinging wildly at her, pulling a knife from under his jacket. She dodged his swing and fell to the ground, rolling over towards the gun lying on the floor. In one quick motion, she picked up the gun, racking a bullet into the chamber and came up with the gun pointed towards Landau. A look of surprise crossed his face, but he still came towards her with the knife. Sabrina did not hesitate, her months of training took over. She held the gun out in a classic two handed stance, and fired off three rounds into Landau's chest. His look of surprise changed as he coughed, dropped the knife and fell to the floor.

Sabrina started shaking. She suddenly realized that she had shot him. She had never shot someone before. "Oh my god! What have I done?" She walked over to the still body on the floor, three small holes in the front of his jacket. Her only thoughts were to get out of there and call the police. She turned and unlocked the small door and headed out of the building. Looking around, she realized she was on the edge of an airport, but she could see some buildings on the distance. She began walking towards the buildings and determined it was a small village. Looking around, she recognized the surrounding land and mountains behind. She was at the bottom of the Appenzell mountains, and she could see the Bodensee in the distance in the other direction, so she was not far from home after-all.

As she reached what looked like main road into the village, several police cars came around the corner, flashing lights and sirens on. She laughed to herself "You're a little too late guys." She turned to flag them down. They were in such a hurry, they almost ran her down. It was the FIS agent in the lead car that recognized her and managed to convince the others to stop.

CHAPTER 33

J ake was bringing up the rear in Helga's VW. He followed the group of police cars because they did not allow him to travel with the police, citing 'too dangerous for civilians', thinking at that time they might have to storm a building. Sabrina tried to convince the police that the danger was over . . . the source of the danger had been eliminated. They were sceptical.

Jake ran to Sabrina, taking her in his arms in a fierce embrace. "Oh my God, Sabrina. I'm so sorry you had to get involved in this . . . I thought I had lost you too."

Sabrina was shaking severely. "Oh Jake, I was so scared! I kept wishing you were with me, and then I kept hoping you'd come to save me . . . and you did!"

"Hell! I didn't save you . . . from what you just told that police officer, it sounds like you handled things all by yourself. What happened?"

Sabrina clutched Jake harder, sobbing violently. "I got him Jake, I got the sonofabitch good."

At that point one of the officers came to them, "Miss Wagner, we'd like you to come with us and show us where you were held . . . which building?"

They walked over to the large warehouse where Sabrina was held. She pointed to the door. "There . . . he's in there." Two of the officers went into the building and were inside for a long time. They came out with confused looks on their faces.

"He's not there . . . there's no body in there Miss Wagner. Are you sure you killed him?"

"What . . . what are you saying? Of course I'm sure, it's not every day I shoot someone. I guarantee, three 9mm. shots to the chest . . . I saw the bullet holes."

They all went in, looking around the large interior. "That's the room back there where I was locked up." She then pointed towards the car. "He dropped right over there by the car, he was trying to get me in the car."

"Well, he's not there now!, and there's no blood stains, so if he was shot . . . he healed up very fast."

Jake was baffled. "How can anyone survive three 9mm. bullets to the chest?"

One of the officers interrupted with "It's quite possible . . . he might have been wearing a vest . . . body armour is quite effective these days."

"Did you find any brass?" Jake asked.

"Yes, we did find three cartridges scattered around where Miss Wagner said it happened."

"Great! said Jake, frustrated beyond belief. "Are you telling me that our friend Landau actually survived and he could be on the loose again . . . and we don't have any idea where he is or where he's going?"

The officer that commented on the body armour added "He might be on the loose, but I guarantee you he will be very sore for a few days."

Kurt Landau was indeed sore. He picked the remaining pieces of the three bullets out of the Kevlar fabric of his vest. His breathing was difficult and he knew he would have some major bruising on his chest for the foreseeable future, but he felt that was better than the alternative. He couldn't believe how that woman had fooled him so easily . . . and move . . . she moved like a cat, knocked him off balance, picked up that gun and handled it like a pro. She had to have training . . . lots of it. He decided he better know his targets a little more before he does something stupid like that. He had miss-read Jake Prescott last year, thinking he was a bumbling amateur scientist, until he discovered that he too was trained in martial arts and weapons handling. This was his second surprise . . . there better not be a third.

His escape from the warehouse building was a stroke of luck. Sabrina had occupied the police long enough for him to leave the building and trek across some fields to the highway for a short distance to the train station at Rheineck. From there he was almost home-free, heading back towards Bregenz. He had no intention of stopping at Bregenz, but carried on to find another village where he could set up his base of operations again.

Jacques Manet called Jake as soon as heard the news. "Jake . . . what the hell are you up to now?" he yelled into the phone. "I thought I told you to leave this to the local police!"

"I did Jacques, honestly . . . and they did a fine job, except that my dear Sabrina was one step ahead of them and shot Landau."

"That's what I heard down here in Lyon. But I also heard that Landau's on the run again . . . what happened?"

Jake filled him in on Sabrina's abduction and subsequent escape, and how she managed to put three bullets into Landau's chest."

"Bloody Hell!" he exclaimed, "is she OK?"

"Yes, a little shaken up, but doing fine . . . probably better than I would have felt. She's one tough cookie . . . I had no idea!" He then added "And to think, the first time I met her, she was filling in for the local preacher in Bregenz . . . then I find she used to be an FIS agent, has all kinds of martial arts training, and can handle firearms with deadly results, as we've seen today."

Jacques laughed. "Sounds like just the kind of girl you need Jake, knowing your track record. It's going to take someone like that to handle the likes of you. God, what a pair! Jake, you know they will want to question her for some time . . . without you present."

"Yes Jacques, the Swiss police have already taken her . . . I think to the St. Gallen office, that's where the Swiss guys were stationed. All this action took place on Swiss soil, except for the actual kidnapping. I think they feel they have more jurisdiction in the case, considering Sabrina was one of them."

"Oh, I'm sure she's in good hands Jake. Don't you have something else you can do?" Jacques was laughing at him, knowing that Jake would be pacing the floor, mumbling about the delays of bureaucracy and red tape.

"Yes Jacques, and I'd better get to it, rather than listen to advice from you!"

It was late evening by the time they returned Sabrina to her home. By that time Scott Anderson and Linda were there, anxiously waiting for news.

Linda ran to Sabrina as she entered the house . . . "My God Sabrina, how are you? Jake has told us some of the news . . . however did you get away? No . . . don't answer that . . . I think I already know. You poor girl!"

"Poor girl, nothing!" countered Scott. "It sounds to me like she handled herself very well . . . perhaps you should feel sorry for Mr. Landau."

They all gathered around, uncertain whether to feel sorry for Sabrina, or stand back in awe. She put their minds at rest by telling of her questioning session with the local Swiss police. "Of course, they knew who he was, they have all been notified by Interpol, and have been watching for him for the past week. It just happened to be me that ran into him."

"Ran into him, my foot!" yelled Jake. "We have to be a little more careful, and little more watchful, and a lot more aware of our surroundings. This guy is very clever, good at disguises, and right now is seeking revenge, so he'll be doubly dangerous."

CHAPTER 34

Jacques Manet was just coming out of a meeting with his own security staff. They had been discussing the recent security breaches and intelligence leakage. They decided that the only person common to all the leaks was the young Serbian translator, Malina Aleksov. Jacques couldn't help but feel there was some connection between this girl and the poison expert they knew was from Serbia. Jacques liked this girl, and was disappointed that she might be involved. She was an excellent translator for several languages, and a hard worker as well. He decided to talk to her, try to find out what her motivation was.

"So, Malina," Jacques started, "I suppose you are wondering why I called you in for this meeting." He paused, noting a sudden change in her demeanor, so he took a chance. "How long have you known Dejana Babić?"

It was a wild guess, but it paid off. The girl just fell apart. "I'm sorry, so sorry. I really like you M. Manet, you have been very kind to me . . . I really didn't want to kill you!"

This came as a shock to Jacques. "Kill me . . . what are you talking about?"

"Dejana . . . you know about her . . . it was she that suggested I kill you . . . I didn't want to do it, but my family . . ."

"Hold on Malina," Jacques started to explain, then decided to let her explain further. "No, actually go ahead and tell me what you know, what your connection is with Dejana."

The girl was in tears now, realizing her career with Interpol could be over, a job she loved.

"Dejana is a distant cousin, a good friend of my family. She helped me get through college in Beograd and suggested I try for a translator job here at Interpol. She was right, I had the skills for the job, and my knowledge of the extra languages because of my parents. I have enjoyed working here for the past few years."

There was a pause, and Jacques did not want to interrupt this amazing confession he was witnessing. "Go ahead, take your time".

"It was after I had worked here for about a year, when I was home on vacation, we were together for someone's celebration, and she asked me how things were, was there anything interesting happening, etc. We talked a little, and I told a few stories about our cases, nothing secret at that time."

"At that time . . .?"

"Yes, it wasn't until some time later she asked me if I ever learned anything more exciting, current emergencies, people we were chasing . . . you know." She stopped.

"And . . ."

"I told her that yes, I knew of things, but I could not discuss them because of security issues. She accepted that at first, but later brought it up again, asking me how much money some of these 'secrets' were worth. And would it really harm anyone if she told somebody?"

"So, she offered you money?"

"Yes, we discussed it in great detail, which items I could possibly pass on, others I would keep, and how much she would pay me, in cash, and how much she would give my family."

"Oh my God, Malina . . . I had no idea. . . so this is what you did?"

"Yes, M. Manet, and I'm ashamed to admit it now." She looked at Jacques, a picture of despair.

"Are you going to arrest me now?" She asked, her lips trembling.

"Not right away Malina . . . I'm still in shock, I have to process all this." He then remembered her first words she had uttered. "But tell me . . . what's this about killing me?"

"Oh God . . . I never should have let it go this far. That man, Landau, the one you were chasing, was almost here with orders to kill you. I learned about your plans to meet and stop him and passed it on to Dejana."

"I was wondering how he caught on so fast."

"And because he did not do the job . . . Dejana asked me to do it . . . for a huge bonus, a bonus that would help my family a lot, even if I was caught or killed." She broke down again, sobbing across the table from Jacques. "I don't think she likes you at all, M. Manet."

"So it appears," commented Jacques dryly, knowing the entire story and all the reasons why Landau did not like him. Jacques thought a bit, an idea forming in his mind. "Malina, I would like you to carry on with your work . . . just as if none of this was discussed. As for what we're going to do with you, I have a lot to think about. I have to have some other meetings, and I'll talk to you later today. Oh, if Dejana contacts you, just stall her, or say you're working on the problem, or whatever."

After Malina left his office, Jacques called another meeting with his security specialist, his computer expert and his immediate boss. As he related the story to them, he watched as they all were amazed and shocked that this had been going on under their noses and not detected. Each one felt a little guilty about their own carelessness, so they were ready when Jacques suggested a solution.

"First, I'd like to say that this girl is only guilty of looking after her family, and being a little naive about the seriousness of her own work, and the data she handles. I am thinking we should turn her around and have her work for us."

"But she already works for us." said somebody who immediately regretted it. "Oh yes, of course . . . I see what you're saying."

"It wouldn't work forever, but maybe we could learn enough in the short term to catch Landau, and maybe get some actionable evidence on this Serbian bitch. Of course, Malina will have to be warned, put on probation or some other punishment to indicate to her she did not get off Scott-free."

They all thought about it and finally relented and agreed that Jacques' plan was good one.

Jacques did not look forward to his next meeting with Malina, but knew she would accept the conditions he was offering. He wished he could discuss this with Jake, as he would have some good advice, and know which way to approach this. Again, he thought it was peculiar that when a difficult situation arose, the first person he thought of was Jake Prescott. He had learned some time ago that Jake had that innate sense of putting it all together, seeing the 'big picture', so to speak.

Jacques then called Annette, his secretary, into the meeting with Malina, after explaining to her what he was trying to do. Annette was also very surprised and interested. It turned out that Malina was delighted and very grateful to be given another chance. She even offered a few suggestions on how she would divert Dejana's attention from some of the details.

"But tell me Malina, how were you planning to kill me . . . or had you figured that out yet?"

"Oh yes," she said as she reached into her purse and pulled out the small glass vial of poison. She then explained what Dejana had told her months ago, and about how dangerous the little vial of poison was.

Jacques reached for the vial. "I think we'll keep that for now, Malina. I want to have it analyzed. Did Dejana tell you how it works, or how I was supposed to die?"

"I think I was supposed to try to put it in your tea or coffee, just a few drops, she said . . . and don't touch it. I think she has used this before . . . and I think that Landau character also has some. Dejana seems to know a lot about poisons.

"Yes, that's her specialty." Jacques said, thinking back on a few of the examples of her handiwork. In his drink . . . probably the same stuff that was used on Heinrich Kohler in Vancouver. What did Jake call it? Batrachotoxin . . . all he could remember was that it was made from poison dart frogs to go on arrows used for hunting. Once again, he realized just how close he had come to his own demise, most likely a very painful end.

CHAPTER 35

Jacques Manet stretched a few rules when he called Jake to set up a conference call between himself, Jake and Jake's staff in Vancouver. "I'm not supposed to be doing this . . . sharing confidential material and internal investigations, but considering the situation, and how involved you guys already are, I feel it's justified. After all, you are the ones under threat, as well as myself."

"What . . . Jacques . . . has your life been threatened as well?" asked Jake.

"Yes, on two counts!" Jacques started. He then explained how Landau had been on his way to Lyon to assassinate him and how Malina had passed on a warning through Dejana.

"Who's Malina?" came the obvious question.

"I was just coming to that." He explained who Malina was and recounted their meetings, as well as her connection with Dejana Babić.

"God!" yelled Jake. "No wonder this guy is always one step ahead of us. I hope you've dealt with her . . . very severely."

"Not exactly, here's what we're planning," Jacques started. I must tell you this in the form of a warning as well, as you are all involved. Any suggestions or comments would be appreciated."

Jacques continued, explaining their plans to turn Malina's employment at Interpol into their own advantage. At first their was a complete silence from them all.

Jake was the first to comment. "sounds like a reasonable approach Jacques . . . but it doesn't really solve any of our problems. We have to gather intelligence on this woman in Serbia . . . some actionable intelligence. We also need an inside line to where Landau is at any given time. We have to stop this guy, before he gets one of us."

Alan interrupted at this point. "Jacques . . . do you know how Landau was going to eliminate you.?"

"Yes . . . it was poison. Malina had a small vial that Dejana gave her . . . most likely the same stuff that was used in Vancouver"

"Batrachotoxin!" yelled Alan. "I suspected as much. I'd love to get my hands on some of that . . . to find out what she's done to make it even more deadly. We only had a few traces on that bottle to work with here."

"I'd love to send you some Alan, but I'm sure the Postal Services in both our countries would not appreciate that. I'll have my lab people talk to you, maybe we can all work together." He then added "Perhaps we can arrange a special courier delivery to you with a small amount of this stuff . . . certainly more than you had before."

They continued to discuss security and the dangers that face them all. "Christ Jacques!" said Jake. "You'd better be careful, this guy is out for both of us, and he wants blood!"

"Don't worry about me Jake, I have an entire police force surrounding me that he has to get through. What do you have?"

Despite the seriousness of the situation, Jake had to chuckle . . . "I've got Sabrina!"

Dejana Babić was furious, frustrated and barely able to control her emotions. Landau had not only failed to get closer to Manet, but had returned to Bregenz and kidnapped Prescott's girl-friend! How stupid can you get? How many times had she warned Landau not to let personal vendettas influence his actions? This was why she had those rules, and how she had survived so long in this dangerous game. Then her girl Malina, was not working out as she had hoped. Dejana was sure she was stalling, not really wanting to complete her task, despite the huge bonus she had been promised.

She would have to have another meeting with her and either convince her, or eliminate her . . . no loose ends. But now she was preoccupied with Landau. She must stop this idiot before he went off on another flight of revenge.

To ease her frustrations, she called Braco, her security guard, into her office. When he arrived, he smiled at her, knowing what was coming . . . the only reason she ever called him into her office.

"Braco . . . how long have we known each other?'

"Many years, Janny," he replied, using his own nickname for her instead of her title, which he normally used.

"Yes, and almost all of that time, you have been a very patient man . . . and an excellent lover."

"I'm glad you think so Janny."

"But even more important, you have been loyal, obedient, faithful, and have stood by me through the good and the bad."

"Yes . . ." he said hesitantly, unsure of what was coming.

"Today . . ." she started, not knowing how she was going to word this. "Today . . . after you make love to me, I want to give you a job to do . . . probably the most important job I have ever given you."

Braco smiled, and wondered at the same time just what this task was she was going to give him. He had accomplished same rather questionable duties in the past, but she had never approached them in this manner. The question provided new excitement to their tryst. He started removing his clothes as he approached her, his eyes devouring her body as he came closer.

Later that day, much later . . . Braco sat in the company library studying some files. Their lovemaking had drained him, in more ways that one. Dejana was a very sexy lady, and a very demanding lover, and their occasional 'meetings' usually ended in both of them exhausted.

When she finally explained this new job she was assigning him, he felt both apprehension and excitement. He had never actually met Landau, but he knew of his reputation and history in the brief time he had worked for his 'Janny'. He knew the type, there were many of them in Serbia and throughout the Balkans and Eastern Europe, remnants left over from the cold war . . . very skilled, highly trained killers, left without a job. But who needs a skilled assassin these days? It turns out there are more than you might think, organizations or individuals who will pay good money for these skills. Skills that are essential for either a bodyguard or special security personnel. These are the knowledge and skills that Dejana had cashed in on for years, skills that had made him so valuable, skills which he must use to prove himself against another of the same type.

His assignment . . . simple . . . just find and kill Kurt Landau . . . as quickly and efficiently as possible. Dejana had some information on the man, a few files in her 'library', with his history . . . as much as she knew, and his work for her in the past year. Not a lot to go on . . . but he would try to absorb everything he could and get into the mind of this ex-Spetsnaz killer, and figure out his next move. Braco had an advantage . . . he too was *Спецназ*, Spetsnaz, and knew few tricks of the trade so-to-speak.

First, he had to know what motivated the man . . . that was easy . . . from what Janny had told him, he was obsessed with his need for revenge, he had to get even with this Canadian scientist and the French Interpol agent. First, the Canadian. He knew he was in Bregenz, originally for a colleague's funeral, now involved with a local girl, a girl that had given Landau the slip, actually shot him with his own gun! He would have to check her out later, she sounded interesting.

From what Janny had mentioned, Landau would probably head back to Bregenz as soon as things settled down. From his own training and experience, Braco knew that Landau would be coming discreetly, in disguise, and very unexpected.

CHAPTER 36

Sabrina was exhausted. After her ordeal with Landau, the adrenaline "high" that had sustained her through the event had finally worn off, dropping her into a severe low. She knew through her training what to expect, but it did nothing to make her feel better. As she recounted the experience, first to the police, then her friends, she began to realize just how close she had come to losing her life. She tried to rationalize her actions, knowing that her training had saved her from disaster, but if she had not had that training, she might not have taken so many chances. Not chances . . . stupid moves!

She felt bad for Jake . . . he was torn between his concern for her safety, and his desire to chew her out and give her hell for being such a hero. The others were in awe of her as she recounted her actions to overcome Landau. She almost laughed at the looks on their faces as she told her story. As the sedative given to her by the doctor finally took over, she pulled the blanket up and dropped into a deep sleep.

Jake had his own problems. Besides the shock and concern he felt for Sabrina, he had to deal with his office in Vancouver. Shannon was on the phone again, "Are you opening an Austria division?" she quipped. "You might as well, you're never here!"

Once again, Jake was reminded how lucky he was to have both the financial backing and the capable crew to keep his Vancouver office alive, and still afford his European excursions and adventures.

"Now Shannon, you know I could leave everything to you guys to run, and you handle things so well." Jake paused, trying to sort all the happenings into a chronological order. "Further to our discussions about Landau and the spy that Babić had in the Interpol office, I guess I haven't told you about Sabrina's run-in with Landau." Jake apologized again and recounted the events of the past couple of days, emphasizing Sabrina's skill at overcoming Landau, as well both the relief and disappointment when she found she had not in fact killed him.

"Oh my God!" Shannon screamed, yelling for her co-workers to come to the phone and listen. "We've been talking to Jacques at Interpol, but we had not heard any of this."

"Well, it really just happened, so Jacques barely knows the details. The worst part is Landau is still on the loose!"

"Jolly good for Sabrina!" Alan exclaimed, "I really want to meet this lady!"

"Well," Jake answered, when that happens, you'd better be careful what you say or do, as she might just dump you on your ass!" Jake stopped, thinking about what Landau could do. "I don't want to alarm you guys, but I think you should have a contingency plan in place to increase your security around there. I doubt if our friend would go to the trouble of traveling to Vancouver to get even with me, but it's a possibility. Keep your wits about you, and don't get sucked in by any ruse."

"No problem Jake, we'll be ready if he tries anything."

"In the meantime Peter, I would like you to do your 'computer' thing, and see what you can find out about our Serbian bitch."

"We've already done that Jake," Peter answered, "We know about as much as we can from the regular sources."

"Well, try some 'irregular' sources . . . you know, do some of your hacking . . . you should be able to do all the things that Interpol are not allowed to do. . . not legally, that is. I want to know everything about her and everyone who works for her now, or did work for her in the past. We already missed this Malina girl at Interpol . . . and although she was not actually employed by Babić, she had history, an association, an old connection. These are the things we have to look for . . . who else does she have that might come after us? I want to know these people before they know us!"

"We understand Jake, we'll try to double our efforts here . . . but for God's sake, please watch out, take care of yourself. And take care of Miss Sabrina . . . we'd really like to meet her!"

Braco stepped down from the train in Bregenz, feeling good to be on a hunt again. His specialty in the Spetsnaz was tracking people down . . . hunting either the enemy, or one of their own that had turned . . . one way or the other. He seldom failed . . . once he studied and learned as much as he could about his prey, he possessed an uncanny ability to anticipate their actions, guess what they would do next. He also had the advantage of knowing something about Landau, he knew what he looked like, his size and some of his habits. Landau knew nothing about him, or even that he was being hunted.

From what Dejana told him about Landau, and his fixation on this Jake Prescott, his need for revenge, he knew Landau would return to Bregenz. It was like honey attracting ants, they couldn't resist returning to the site. He just had to make sure Landau got stuck in the honey . . . and he had to make it a fatal attraction.

The first thing Braco did was to rent a car, a small non-descript vehicle that did not attract attention or stand out in a crowd. That way, Jake, or anyone else would barely notice him, and definitely not remember him. He looked at his list of locations, and started to drive around, learning the city and where Jake was staying,

He had two small bags, one light one with a few clothes, and the other very heavy, loaded with the 'tools of his trade'. Tucked away in a safe place, he also had a couple of small vials of poison which Janny had given him before he left.

"Be very careful of this Braco," she said, "I know poison is not your favourite weapon, but there are times . . . just a drop or two . . . and don't touch it!"

As he drove around the first day, he checked out some of the hotels and B&B's in the area, trying to figure out where Landau might stay when he does show up. He checked into a modest hotel and settled in for an unknown time period. Of course, he had no guarantee that Landau would even return to Bregenz, but Braco's hunter sense told him he would be back, he knew Landau's need for revenge would be the driving force.

On the second day he dropped by the tourist office, but the girl called Sabrina was not working. He was a little disappointed, as he wanted to see what was attracting the Prescott guy. He did not return to the tourist office as he knew too many visits would trigger suspicions, or at least create a memory, something he wanted to avoid.

He spent the rest of the evening checking and cleaning his weapons. He then packed them back into their case, placing it in the closet to keep from the prying eyes of the hotel staff . . . everything except a small Beretta handgun, which he tucked under his arm in a discreet holster.

His next challenge was to find where this Prescott fellow was staying, the most likely place where Landau would show up. It did not take long, as Dejana had provided him with enough information. He drove past the house twice, just to confirm the address, then returned to the hotel to decide what his next move was.

CHAPTER 37

Scott Anderson was at a loss for words. In his business as a reporter, that was a serious problem. He turned to Linda and said "I can't believe it Linda! I told Jake yesterday that I could probably make a career out of just following him around. I don't know whether he just anticipates trouble, or creates it. The same thing happened last year when I first met Jake. We hardly had time to get to know each other and he was off to Europe. When I followed, he ended up on a river barge cruising up the Main River, was then attacked by mercenaries." He shook his head, and continued his story, knowing Linda had heard it all before. Scott did this quite often, repeating a story several times, sometimes just to himself, to review the events and get the entire thing clear in his own mind. This way, when he actually wrote it down, the words came easily and naturally.

He continued "I finally caught up to him in a hospital in a small town in Germany. That was just the beginning . . . the beginning of a hair-raising adventure into Bavaria which ended up in a deadly shoot-out." He paused, his face suddenly very sad as he recalled the events of that day.

"I just hope that Jake hasn't opened up another can of worms . . . but it sure sounds like it!"

Linda answered "I can't believe what happened to Sabrina! She seemed like a very nice, sweet young thing . . . who knew she was a deadly, well trained FIS agent."

"It's a good thing she had that training. I think she really is 'a sweet young thing' as you called her, she just is a little more capable than most. Jake is certainly taken by her . . . I hesitate to think what would happen to Jake if anything happened to Sabrina. He's already been through that with Christa last year."

Linda nodded, knowing the story of how Jake's girlfriend, Christa, was gunned down in that deadly shoot-out. Gunned down by Kurt Landau!

Kurt Landau had just arrived back to Bregenz. He couldn't help it . . . the need for revenge had more than doubled after his latest screw-up with Sabrina. He couldn't believe the way she had retaliated, disarming him and shooting him with his own gun! He had dropped his guard, totally not expecting such a skillful response. He would not let that happen again . . . those kind of mistakes could be deadly, and would have been if had not worn his vest, something he didn't always do. He could still feel the bruises on his chest, and it was just getting easier to breathe.

He really hadn't developed a plan yet, nothing firm. He knew this was not a good way to start, but he felt he had to at least come to Bregenz a be ready to move. His last correspondence with Dejana was not amiable. She was furious with him, and in a way, he didn't blame her. She had warned him not to bring personal vendettas into the game, but he obviously had thrown all those rules out the window. What did she know? Dejana couldn't possibly understand the loss he had suffered, the pain and embarrassment caused by this nosey but very clever Canadian scientist . . . this Jake Prescott! So now, he just ignored her text messages and emails, and did not answer her phone calls. She knew he was returning to Bregenz, a fact that infuriated her more, knowing that he was just defying her . . . carrying on with his own agenda regardless of what she wanted.

His own agenda? He didn't have one . . . and he knew he better come up with a plan very soon, before somebody spotted him and he would lose his advantage. He had checked into a small guest house on the edge of town . . . a different one than last time.

As he nursed a healthy glass of his favourite brandy, he reviewed his options. He knew where Sabrina lived, but knew he'd better not go near there, just in case he was spotted. He still did not know where Prescott was staying. He wasn't even sure if he was living with his girlfriend. He decided to do some research and fill in the blanks. He also knew he had to be extra careful, as he had already spotted a few extra police agents hanging around the train station and the tourist office. During his career, he had learned how to spot these guys, no matter how innocent they appeared.

It was just by chance that Scott and Linda were walking around town and spotted Landau as he entered a small mini-market near his guest house.

"Stop!" whispered Scott. "Did you see that guy . . . that guy that just went into the store?"

"No o o o o," answered Linda, "Who?"

"Wait . . . just wait here, don't stare . . . look at something else."

Scott knew that Landau would not recognize him, as he they had never met, and he would not have any idea that a noted WBC reporter would be wandering around Bregenz.

Scott suddenly said to Linda "Here . . . stand here and look at those items in the shop window. I'll tell you when to turn and smile at me."

Within a few minutes, Landau exited the mini-mart and looked up and down the street. In the meantime, Scott had taken out his phone and was composing a photo of Linda . . . typical tourist pose, etc. "That's perfect honey" he said out loud as he snapped a few photos, just managing to catch Landau in the background.

They did not waste any time, turning and walking away quickly . . . on to another tourist attraction. They stopped halfway down the block, checking to see where Landau had gone. They didn't dare try to follow him, knowing just how dangerous that could be. They stopped at a little sidewalk bistro for a coffee, Scott anxious to look at his photos again. "Good!" he exclaimed, "We got the sonofabitch!" With that, he sent the photos to Jake, then dialed his number to talk to him.

CHAPTER 38

F BI Special Agent Bert Jackson was slowly digging himself out of a pile of paperwork. He often thought about the public perception of FBI agents as an exciting, action filled life, running around arresting bad guys on a daily basis. In fact it involved lots of legwork, analyzing tons of boring detail for small bits of information, and above all, piles and piles of paperwork. Bert was good at his job, even the paperwork. The tall African American agent had built a reputation on hard work, experience and an innate intuition that had served him well.

As he reached the last of the paper that had accumulated in the past few days, he spotted a note from Interpol As he glanced over it, he muttered "Damn! This should have been at the top of my pile, not the bottom!" He reached over to the intercom "Jane, could you come in here please . . . and bring in everything you've received from Interpol in the past few days."

Before long, Jane arrived with a rather thin file, placing it on his desk. "Is that all there is?" he asked.

"That's all you want to see just now Bert." she said, knowing where his interest was. "There are a few more things from Interpol, but I know those reports are the ones you want."

At first, Bert was a little confused, until he looked at the first report. The name "Landau" jumped out at him. "Oh my God! What's this guy been up to now?" He opened the file and started reading. The first sheet was a complete, detailed report covering the kidnapping of Sabrina Wagner in Bregenz, Austria, and her subsequent escape. "Holy Sh . . .!" he exclaimed. "Jane . . . did you read this?" he yelled.

"Of course Bert . . . you know I have to read all those reports. I thought that one would catch your eye." She paused, then added "And what's not in the report is that Sabrina . . . the kidnapping victim, is Jake Prescott's new girlfriend."

"Wha . . . how'd you find that out?"

"I have my sources . . . she laughed. "Actually, I talked with Jacques Manet at Interpol . . . he's quite familiar with this incident, and I think you should talk with him asap."

"Good idea . . . could you please get him on the phone?" He glanced at his watch "He should still be at work, it's only late afternoon there. In the meantime, I'll look at the rest of these reports."

He didn't get very far when he came across another report telling him that Landau had just returned to Bregenz and all the law authorities were on alert. "Jesus H christ! What is this guy up to?"

"Jacques Manet is on line one." announced Jane.

"Jacques!" he almost yelled. "What the hell is going on in Bregenz? And what's Landau doing back there? Can't the local cops pick him up?"

"And hello to you Bert . . . nice to hear from you." a sarcastic reply came back.

"Oh sorry Jacques, of course, hello and how are you? The last time we talked . . . you guys were in Paris, talking with that Marcel Bergeron, just as he was killed if I remember correctly. I just got through a pile of paperwork and discovered these reports about our friend in Bregenz. That all sounds pretty serious."

"It is Bert, and I'm quite worried about it. To make it even worse, we have a bunch of amateurs wandering around, getting in the way of things. The problem is . . .it is their presence that is attracting the bad guys, sort of a catalyst to start this reaction."

Bert thought a moment, then said "And I suppose our Canadian friend is right in the middle of it?"

"Well of course! . . . He's the cause of it all . . . Landau is out to get him . . . one way or another. He still hasn't forgotten that fiasco in Bavaria last year, where all his grand plans were stripped away by some Canadian scientist. It was Jake again this time who figured out what killed that guy in Vancouver, and who was behind it!" He stopped briefly, then added with a laugh "We might be better off if we locked up Jake . . . used him as bait." He continued "And if you read further, there is probably a report in there about a Serbian woman, the one we think is behind all these poisonings, operating as sort of support for Landau. We think she was also behind the poisoning of Marcel Bergeron in Paris, through another of her 'agents'."

"Oh my God . . . here we go again!" he remembered much of the events of the previous year, and especially the actions of Kurt Landau. He still had warrants out for Landau and persons unknown for the actions leading to the deaths of sixty-one people in two different traffic poisoning attacks, the explosive demise of an NSO agent, and the assassination of a US Senator. Almost all of these had indirect links to Landau, whom they had no trace of for the past year.

"So when did he reappear?" Bert asked.

"As far as we can tell, when that scientist was killed in Vancouver. You should have another report on that . . . it was Jake Prescott who identified both the victim, whom he knew, and the perpetrator, Landau, from the CCTV footage from the hotel."

"I'd really like to get my hands on this guy!"

"You and me both" answered Jacques.

"So what are your plans Jacques . . . what are the local police up to?"

"The Austrian police are on alert, If they can find him while he's in Bregenz, they'll get him. Just so you know, the Swiss FIS is also on site . . . or at least nearby. That girl, Sabrina, used to be one of them, a fully trained FIS agent . . . much to Landau's surprise! That's probably how she escaped. Too bad Landau had that vest on, we might have been finished with him. He probably won't make that mistake again. But remember, Landau is a slippery character, very skilled at what he does . . . good training, excellent at disguises, knows his way around and knows how law enforcement works."

Bert agreed, trying to think how he or the FBI could help. "We want this guy as much as you do Jacques . . . now that he has reappeared, I think I'll come over . . . I might be able to offer some support, if only another set of eyes."

"Jolly good Bert!" answered Jacques. "I was hoping you would offer . . .I haven't worked with one of your FBI blokes for a couple of years. I always admired the skills you guys bring to the table . . . of course you realize I can't be there . . . but I'll be in touch."

"I'll let you know when I can be there." Bert replied as he signed off.

"Jane . . . could you see how soon I can fly out to Bregenz, Austria . . .?"

"Already done, Bert. You're on a flight this evening to Zurich, Switzerland. You can drive from there. I checked Prescott's crew in Vancouver . . . apparently that's the best route. I'll explain it to you."

CHAPTER 39

Jake was at Sabrina's house when the call came in from Scott. The photo was a good one, clearly showing his nemesis Kurt Landau exiting from the minimart with a small bag of groceries.

Jake stared at it for a long time, mesmerized by this monster that had impacted his life so much.

"Hello . . . Hello? Are you still there Jake?" Scott was yelling over the phone.

"Yeah, of course Scott . . . sorry, I got hung up staring at this photo. You were lucky to get it, thanks for sharing . . . I'll send it to Jacques at Interpol."

"Good . . . and Jake . . . I think we should get together right away . . . now we know Landau is right here. We have to come up with some plans, action plans or contingency plans . . . something to keep us all safe . . . as you know, this guy is deadly!"

"Good idea Scott . . . but don't you believe the police have this under control?"

"Not for a minute!"

A short time later, Jake showed the photos to Sabrina and Helga, then emailed them to Jacques at Interpol. Sabrina shuddered as she viewed the pictures. "That's him alright," she whispered,

"I'm sorry Jake , , , just looking at these pictures brings back some scary memories."

"I can't blame you Sabrina. I feel the same way . . . every time I look at him, I see the face firing towards us amid smoke and steam in that cabin."

Helga interrupted with "OK, we know how bad he is . . . what are we going to do to prepare for the day he arrives at our doorstep?"

"Right, I agree Helga, I think we should talk to the local police, they might have some ideas. In the meantime, Sabrina, can you show me what you have in this house for the extra security you mentioned."

"OK, first Helga has her weapons both here and at her place."

Helga interrupted with "Yes, Jake, that's a couple of 9mm Berettas with full magazines."

Sabrina added "and I have my FIS Glock 9mm and my own little Beretta Pico, which I will be carrying from now on."

"God, I can't believe this is happening!" Jake exclaimed. "And I'll have my Sig Sauer 9mm! Jesus! We have enough fire-power to start a war."

"We might need it." was the answer.

At that point, there was a knock on the door, startling them all. Jake had his gun out of the holster, as Sabrina answered the door, welcoming Scott Anderson and Linda.

"Christ!" yelled Jake, "We just have to be careful we don't shoot each other."

Scott was stopped at the doorway. "Ahem . . . guys . . . Sabrina . . . could you come and tell your guards that we're on your side?"

Sabrina was already there, talking to the two men outside in German. She then turned to explain "Sorry guys . . . those two are the security that have been assigned to watch the house . . . watch over me so-to-speak. They are both men I used to work with at FIS." she turned to Jake and said "To answer your question Jake, that's part of the security we have here . . . anyone approaching the house gets checked out."

Kurt Landau was watching this from a distance, his binoculars covering the area in front of Sabrina's house. "Damn!" he muttered, looks like she's got a couple of baby-sitters . . . experienced ones by the look of it." After his many years in the security business he could see that these two men knew what they were doing, appeared capable, and were well armed. "I guess I'll have to try a different approach." he thought, already forming an alternate plan.

He never had a chance to try his alternate plan. As he approached his car, he dropped his guard and was looking down, replacing his binoculars into their case. A massive blow struck him from behind, almost knocking him out. He staggered, trying to turn to see who or what his assailant was. He barely had a chance before another powerful blow hit him, driving him back against the car. He tried to reach for his gun, but something smashed his arm, excruciating pain telling him it was broken. He dropped to the ground, trying to cover himself from further blows. A couple of kicks to his side knocked the breath out of him, cracking his ribs. He knew he had to retaliate to survive, somewhere in the back of his mind he knew this was a targeted attack, something he had seen done many times, and as he drifted into unconsciousness, he wondered who was behind it. One more blow to the head, and everything went black.

Luckily, someone had seen part of the attack and was calling for help.

He very slowly regained consciousness in the hospital. He groaned as he tried to move, or turn over. The pain was as bad as he could remember and he could scarcely breathe. Slowly, he discovered he had one arm in a cast and the other arm handcuffed to the side of the bed. They obviously were not taking any chances, so they must know who he was, he thought.

Guten Morgen, Herr Landau. Good morning, Mr. Landau." a voice came to him. He struggled to turn enough to see who was talking.

A uniformed police officer stood at the foot of his bed, a well armed police officer. "It looks like you ran across some bad luck last night. Someone didn't like your appearance and decided to change it . . . not much better in my opinion." he smiled. With that, he turned and left the room.

Almost immediately, another man entered the room. This one had a different uniform with a small Swiss insignia on a shield crest. Landau was a little confused. Why are the Swiss authorities involved?" Then it struck him "Of course! That girlfriend of Prescott . . . no wonder she was so good, she must have had FIS training!" He decided to shut up, let them work at whatever they want . . . all he wanted to do right now was rest.

"No, no, no Herr Landau! You are not going to have the luxury of sleeping. You must stay awake, this is going to be an exciting time for you! So many people want to come and see you, want to talk to you, and of course, they want you to talk to them." He paused a moment, waiting for Landau to open his eyes. "And just to make it more exciting, we're not going to give you any pain meds . . . no drugs . . . we'd like you to be wide awake during the entire procedure . . . we have to know all about your recent activities."

Sabrina's guards heard the news before they did. One of them came in to talk to Sabrina just before the phone rang with the news. Apparently they were right, Landau had been watching them with binoculars from a location not far away. "Jesus! I knew it!" exclaimed Jake. "So all our precautions were justified!"

Once they received the details of the attack, more questions surfaced. "Who did this? Who has the motivation and the skills to catch Landau unawares enough to beat him within an inch of his life? If a local resident hadn't come along, he probably would have been dead."

It was only the following morning they had some of their questions answered. One of Sabrina's friends from the FIS dropped by to give her the information. Sabrina explained to him who everyone was and their involvement with Landau. For this reason, he was comfortable enough to disclose all of the information he had on the attack.

"Apparently the guy was big . . . and powerful. He caught Landau off guard and beat the shit out of him. Broke his arm with a club of some kind, and kicked in his ribs. They think the last kick knocked him out . . . just before that guy came along and called the police and ambulance. He's lucky to be alive."

"Yeah, we know," Jake added, "but he has lots of lives . . . he's lost several already."

The police officer looked a little puzzled, but did not ask any more questions.

"But you don't know anything about his assailant?" asked Scott. "Surely he can't disappear that fast, and that effectively?" His reporter instinct was taking over, wanting some answers.

"No," answered the policeman, "but he must have been good . . . I mean smart and very tough."

Jake's sense of *deja-vu* tickled him. "I think we've seen this before, only different. I don't know who, but somebody wants Landau dead! . . . someone besides us I mean." laughing at his own wry humour.

Braco Dragonović sat in a bar, nursing a drink and licking his wounds . . .not wounds to his body, just to his ego. He had managed to track down his prey easily enough, then catch him unawares enough to really hurt him. If that guy hadn't come along at the wrong time, he would have finished the job. He knew he had to be a little smarter to finish the job now, Landau would have lots of police around him, so it would not be as easy to sneak up on him. He also knew he could not report back to Dejana until the job was finished.

Although it really wasn't his style. He pulled out the little vial that Dejana had given him to use if the opportunity came up. He knew Dejana had used this method many times to eliminate her enemies, but Braco preferred the direct approach . . . track down your prey and beat the shit out of him. Poison always seemed to be cheating . . . a woman's style. But, you never know, he thought as he wrapped up the vial again and tucked it back in his pocket.

CHAPTER 40

Jacques Manet couldn't believe his eyes as he read the latest report from Bregenz. They actually had Landau in custody, but apparently there were other things at play, things they had not counted on. He knew that the Austrian authorities and especially the Swiss FIS agents on hand would manage to squeeze some information out of Landau.

Then he asked himself "What information are you expecting?" Realizing they had been concentrating on catching Landau, not analyzing his motives and his end-game. They knew about the Serbian woman, or at least a little bit about her, but they had no idea how Landau fitted into that story, how the whole thing came together, what the 'big picture' looked like.

He then thought of Jake . . . if anyone can see the big picture, it was Jake Prescott. He hit his intercom button. "Annette, could you please try to track down Jake Prescott for me?" He knew he could get little more information from Jake than what appeared on the report.

As soon as Jake saw who was calling, he motioned for the rest of them to gather around, and put the phone on speaker mode, "Hello Mr Manet . . . I suppose I could guess why you are calling?"

"God Jake, I just saw the initial report, you've actually got the son-of-a-bitch in custody?"

"Not us Jacques . . . the Austrian and Swiss authorities, most likely with thanks to you for the help in tracking him. Believe me when I say that if he were in our custody, he most likely would not be alive now. Those Austrian and Swiss police are a little more lenient . . . and they are bound by rules and laws. I'd be tempted to turn him over to Sabrina, so she could finish the job!"

Jacques laughed at this, knowing full well that there was an element of truth in what Jake was telling him. "So what happens now?" he asked.

"You tell me . . . what are you, or the authorities planning to do with him?"

"Well as far as Interpol is concerned, we've helped with the first stage, now the local authorities that have him will have to decide the next step. I know Bert Jackson and the FBI would really like to have him back in the States to face God knows how many charges of murder and mayhem. But . . . I think first for you and I, Jake, we have to find out who this other guy is and how he fits into the picture. We have a good idea what motivated Landau . . . that's you . . . but we don't know who else is involved. And then there's this Serbian woman . . . how is she involved . . . or is she? I thought you might have some ideas or answers . . . you seem to be good at that Jake"

"Well, I'll tell you Jacques, I'm not sure this will help our case. First, from what I've learned from the FIS guys here . . . you're not going to get much out of Landau. He's ex-Spetsnaz, for God's sake. These guys don't give up anything they don't want to . . . it doesn't matter what you do to him. From what they're telling me, he's already hurting pretty bad from his beating, so anything you do to him won't matter."

"Who was it did this . . . do they have any idea?"

"Well, from what they got from the witness, the guy who phoned it in . . . he's a big guy, very strong, very fast. He must also be very clever . . . actually tracked down Landau when we couldn't. It's a possibility that he's ex-Spetsnaz as well. They had guys that were especially trained to track people down and deal with them, so-to-speak." Jake paused, thinking about what Jacques had asked him. "As far as the 'big picture' is concerned Jacques, there is a possibility that the Serbian woman is involved with this . . . maybe Landau was working for her. Maybe this big assassin is also her guy, sent to deal with Landau. Maybe she doesn't like Landau spending all his time trying to even with me . . . to her it is non-productive time, she's not making any money on it. Just too many 'maybe's' Jacques."

"Wow! I hadn't thought of that Jake. That's probably as good a theory as any right now. I have a feeling it's all linked, I just don't know how. We're still trying to find actionable links from any of these deaths back to the Serbian woman. Other than our 'resident assassin', as I now call our translator, Malina, she is the only person who has positive links to the Serbian . . . which worries me a little, it makes her very vulnerable if the bitch figures out that we know about that link."

Dejana already knew that Landau had been captured and was in custody in the hospital in Bregenz. She had very little information on his condition, but suspected if Braco had caught up with Landau, he most likely wasn't in very good shape. What puzzled her was she had not heard anything from Braco, but figured he would not contact her until he finished the job. She sent out a couple more text messages, not only to Braco, but a few other contacts that might provide additional information.

She sat back, trying to enjoy her only vice, other than sex, her large snifter of Courvoisier Cognac. Her entire world, a world which she had kept so private for so many years, was closing in on her, too many loose ends. Ever since that screw-up in Paris when that idiot spilled the beans just before he was eliminated. She would have to be more careful in selecting her 'staff', as she liked to call them.

And then there was Malina, her favourite, who was well ensconced in Interpol as a translator. It proves you should never involve your family . . . even distant family. She had missed her last assignment, the only one she ever been given. In addition, she was ignoring Dejana's texts. Either she had been discovered, or they were monitoring her phone for some reason. In that case, Dejana could understand why Malina was not trying to communicate.

So many little problems . . all adding up to one thing . . . it was time to hit the 'pause button'. Time for her to pull back, protect herself before this got out of control. For many years, she had operated alone, or with very limited assistance. This had worked for her very well. She had total control of every part of the operation, every action that was taken, so any corrective action that was needed, she could handle it immediately. Now, there was too much of a time lag between what was happening, and what action had to be taken. Things were better then, but her operation grew, and with that growth came the inevitable problems of growth. It was at that time she knew she had to protect herself in the future.

She had a plan, one she had developed years before, a sort of 'back-up' plan, or a 'cover-your-ass' plan. She figured it was now time to implement that plan. As she finished her cognac, she sent out a blanket text message to all her 'staff', basically telling them to shut down, halt all operations, go to ground, do not communicate in any way until further notice. She felt by cutting off all connections with her operators, she could isolate herself from any further exposure. This might have worked at one time, but she forgot she was living in a digital age when data does not disappear completely, just because you turn off the machine.

Unknown to Dejana, thousands of miles away, a young Chinese-Canadian by the name of Peter Wong was typing furiously away at his computer, watching the entire 'shut-down' operation that Dejana thought was so secure. Eventually, he turned and picked up the phone.

CHAPTER 41

"Good morning Shannon", Jake answered the phone on the first ring. "What time is it in Vancouver, and why are you in the office?"

"Well Boss," she joked, "Somebody has to keep the home-fires burning, so-to-speak. Peter's come up with something that he thinks you should know . . . here he is."

"Jake, hello? How are things in Europe? Where the hell are you now?"

"Still in Bregenz, Austria, Peter. Thanks for helping Shannon hold the fort. She says you have something for me?"

"I might have something interesting . . . it's about the Serbian bitch, Dejana Babić, I've been 'investigating' some of her recent activities."

"So, what have you discovered?"

"She's a very interesting woman, very secretive, very difficult to find anything on line that might compromise her in any way. She's normally very cautious, very cautious indeed, but she must be getting a little nervous, because she just sent out word to her entire networks of contacts to shut down her whole operation. I think Jake, she's caught wind of you guys poking around, and she's gone to ground."

"Well that's interesting," said Jake, "Between the activity at Interpol and the problems here with Landau, I'm not surprised she's getting a little suspicious."

"Yes, I hear you've caught Landau . . . good work!"

"Well, no, we haven't caught him, the Austrians and Swiss have him . . . and . . . wait a minute . . . there's something you could do Peter . . . both you and Alan. Could you check any contacts you have that is familiar with or was part of the Russian Spetnaz organization. I'd like to know anything we can learn about their training, particularly with respect to interrogation techniques, control, avoidance, . . . anything at all that might help to get some information out of this guy."

"Good, I think I know what you want. I'll ask Alan to check out his sources as well."

"And . . ." added Jake, "See what you can find out about this big, tough guy that beat the shit out of Landau. Although in one way I'd like to give him a medal, we would really like to know if he's working for Dr. Babić, or was one of Landau's old enemies, and just who he is . . . after all, he's still on the loose, not someone we'd like to bump into on the streets."

"Good, we'll see what we can find out."

Kurt Landau was licking his wounds. Serious wounds. He groaned as he tried to turn over to relieve the pressure on his broken ribs. Knives of pain shot through his side, making him gasp, which caused another stab of unbearable pain. But bear it he must. They had immobilized his good arm, so both arms were now handcuffed together and to the bed rail, it was difficult to move enough to ease any pain. In a way, he welcomed the pain . . . he used it . . . it kept him awake, aware, and fuelled his anger. His captors watched him closely, but as time wore on and they got nothing out of him, their attention lagged a little, something he was hoping for and counting on. They were smart, they had removed everything useful from him, his gun first of course, but also his keys, his wallet and ID, his pocket-knife, lighter, spare change, a pen . . . anything that could possible be used as a weapon or give him an advantage.

He tried to look around the room to assess his situation as often as he could without his captors seeing what he was doing. It was a small room, a little different from a normal hospital room . . . obviously set up to hold prisoners for short periods of time. Little touches like the bed bolted to the floor, rails to hold handcuffs, bars on the windows, frosted glass, only one door, and that was heavy duty steel, and CCTV cameras monitoring the entire room. The only thing missing was a toilet, a common fixture in a prison cell, but not common in a hospital room. So that told him he was in a modified hospital room, rather than a prison. This could make things a lot easier, he thought, not looking forward to what came next.

His only advantage he had discovered so far was they had handcuffed his hands together palm to palm, something that an expert would not do. Locking hands back to back made things much more difficult to escape from. He inspected the cuffs as much as he could, recognizing them as a standard brand, commonly used by law enforcement.

He flexed his fingers of his right hand. He could feel the special ring that encircled the ring finger, a beautifully fashioned snake, which appeared to be coiled around his finger about three times. It was a lovely piece of jewelry, fashioned by an expert silversmith in Istanbul. He was glad they had not removed it from his hand as he needed it now. Cautiously, with his movements covered by both hands, he worked his other fingers around to manipulate the ring. It was in fact, a long piece of silver that had been fashioned so it looked like a snake wrapped around his finger. He managed to unwind the strip . . . it was a lot harder than he thought, but eventually, he held a long strip of silver in his closed hand. He then manipulated this silver wire over to the handcuff and inserted the thin end into a hole in the cuff. By bending it over, he made a ninety degree bend on the wire, about one centimetre from the end. Slipping the bent end into the keyhole of the cuffs, he carefully turned his little tool, feeling it depress the triple ratchet within the lock . . . the other end of the cuff sprung open. Quickly, he manoeuvred the other hand over and unlatched it. He palmed his little tool and placed his hand over the open cuffs. He then waited for his opportunity.

Braco approached the hospital carefully. It wasn't difficult to find out where they were holding Landau, but to get access to him would be difficult. He didn't know just how much information that witness had passed on, just how much they knew about him, so he couldn't just walk in and try to pass himself off as family or a friend. Because Landau was a fugitive in police custody, that wouldn't have worked either. No, he had to come up with a better plan, so he just found a good location to watch the hospital, the comings and goings to figure out his next step. By late afternoon, he decided he was going into the cleaning business.

It didn't take him long to establish his business. Going to a hardware store at a remote end of town, he bought some white coveralls similar to what he had seen entering the hospital. He also bought a couple of modern sweeping mops, something that would look reasonable for the job. A white painters cap finished his disguise. He knew that people tend to see what they expect to see. As long as you can act the part, and boldly walk in as if you did it every day, nobody would question you. The next step would be the hardest, actually entering the building . . . but he had a plan for that too.

CHAPTER 42

J acques Manet couldn't wait any longer . . . he had to find out what was happening, not just remotely, but by actually being there. Remembering how much trouble he got into last summer, he cleared it with his superior first, saying he had to go to Bregenz to be present at the interrogation of the fugitive they had been tracking for a year. It didn't take much convincing as they were all anxious to hear about Mr. Kurt Landau.

"Annette . . . how long do you think it would take me to get to Bregenz?"

"Well, Mr. Manet, it depends on how fast you drive. Forget flying, trains would take too long for that distance, but if you take the right routes, driving would be about five or six hours, less if you push it."

"Good, I can do that. Could you please call Jake again, tell him I'm on my way." Apparently their interrogation hasn't produced anything of use. Our experts feel that if either Jake or myself were present, it would annoy Landau enough to cut loose with some information. In any case, we'll both show up and see what his reaction is. "Ask Jake to book me somewhere to stay, but I want to be there to see this guy questioned."

"Yes Sir, will do."

Jacques picked up his small travel bag he kept in his office, and was out the door within minutes, excited to be on the road again.

The short text from Peter came through while they were having dinner. Jake had expected some information from Peter, but this message alarmed him even more that he expected. Most likely Peter got the same feeling. He read it out to the others. "Most of the data we have gathered on Landau is same as before, however, most contacts in the business have emphasized the following: 'Do not, repeat, do not trust this man alone . . . he is trained and is highly skilled at escape techniques . . . a regular Houdini!'."

Jake looked at the others around the table, each with their own thoughts. Various looks of either puzzlement or horror crossed their faces. Jake had a sudden sense of *déja vu* and a sinking feeling in his stomach as he realized the significance of that text. Remembering that Landau had escaped from them several times already, he realized just how dangerous this situation could be.

"Sabrina . . . quickly, talk to your guys outside and tell them about this warning. Have them check with the hospital and put double guards on Landau. We don't want that son-of-a-bitch to escape again!"

Sabrina ran to the door to pass on this information. Jake waited for a long time and she didn't return. Walking over to the door, he met Sabina on the way back, her face white. She was shaking as Jake grabbed her. "He's escaped! All hell's broken loose at the hospital. There's already one man dead, another injured."

"My God . . ." as he grabbed for his gun which wasn't there.

"Jake Prescott!" scolded Sabrina . . . "just forget it . . . you're not taking your gun, you stay out of this, let the experts deal with it."

"But . . ."

"No buts . . . if we go anywhere near the hospital, it will be after they have him in custody again, maybe we might get some different answers from him."

Jake calmed down, then turned to Helga, who had joined them for dinner. "Helga . . . could you please book rooms for both Jacques Manet and also Bert Jackson from the F.B.I." He laughed to himself as he thought Scott Anderson and Linda were already staying there, pretty soon they would have the entire hotel booked. "Where is Scott . . . does anyone know?"

"Yes, Linda just sent me a text . . they are both right near the hospital. Scott wanted to go in and interview somebody when they heard shots. They definitely know what's happening. Trust Scott to be on scene to cover the news!"

"Good God! I think we should go there at least to keep Scott and Linda company. This is beginning to sound familiar. Bert Jackson and Jacques Manet are also on their way . . . it's a good thing they aren't here already, we could have a real gunfight at the OK Corral. They probably have enough police officers there to control it."

"Let's hope so!"

Meanwhile, at the hospital, things were not as expected. The entire wing had been shut down, extra security called out, as well as local police and even a few FIS agents to help. The code alarms had sounded for a period, deafening everyone, making it almost impossible to communicate. Shortly after, someone killed the alarms, and a false sense of peace descended on the scene.

Jake and Sabrina found Scott and Linda nearby, talking with an F.I.S. agent who appeared to be in charge. "What's the situation now?" asked Sabrina, speaking to the officer in the Swiss German dialect they both used.

"Well," answered the agent, looking a little embarrassed, "we're not quite sure. We thought it was just this Landau character we were dealing with, but there's somebody else in there, and it appears he was the one that triggered this whole thing. We're still trying to assess the situation, so standby."

Landau heard a noise outside his room, some scuffling, then a couple of muffled shots. "What the hell?" he thought. His guard was also distracted and went out the door to see what was happening, so he took advantage of the lapse in attention to quickly slip his hands out of his cuffs, and slide out of bed. Sharp pains stabbed through his side and down his leg. He ignored the throbbing in his broken arm and shuffled over to the door to see what was going on. Another crash outside and the guard staggered through the door into the room and fell to the floor, he head bleeding. Landau slipped over to one side of the doorway, just in time as a huge man in white coveralls came crashing in behind the guard. He had a gun in one hand and a large club-like weapon in the other. Landau had seen enough of his type to instantly recognize him as Spetsnaz. He knew he was in trouble, this guy was much larger, younger and probably more fit than he was. He also figured that this was the guy that put him in the hospital the day before.

Before Braco had a chance to assess the room, Landau attacked, swinging a chair across the man's face and body with all the strength he could muster. It hurt him almost as much as it hurt his attacker. Braco dropped his club, but swung the gun around to deal with his opponent. He noted Landau's condition, and smiled. "*Guten abend, Herr Landau.* Good evening Mr. Landau. You are looking fine this evening. I would suggest you back off and listen. I have a message from a certain lady we both know." His aim towards Landau did not waver.

Landau knew exactly who he was referring to. Dejana Babić. "So what has Dr. Babić have to say today?" asked Landau, frantically stalling for time as he tried to figure out a way out of this situation "So, are you her messenger boy, her personal assistant, or just a sex object?"

He could see the anger rising in the man's face, obviously he had touched a sensitive subject.

"Don't you talk about Janny that way" he blurted.

"Oh . . . Janny is it . . .?" teased Landau, "How lovely." It was working, he could see Braco's face getting redder. Memories of his training flooded back . . . "don't let your opponent mess with your head, control your temper!"

Braco had enough. He levelled his gun one more time and opened fire.

CHAPTER 43

By the time Jake and his crew had arrived at the hospital, things appeared quiet. Sabrina again talked to one of the police officers to find out what was happening. The answer was not what they were expecting. "We're not sure, there haven't been any shots for at least a a half hour, but nobody had gone in or come out."

"Well," she asked, "hasn't the emergency response team gone in?" She was referring to the local SWAT team to handle these type of situations.

"No . . . they've been tied up with something over in Feldkirch . . . every available man was called in for that situation. What we have here are just local police and some of your guys from the F.I.S. From the shots we heard earlier, we don't know which of the perps is still alive . . . or if either of them is. And we don't know what other casualties there might be."

Sabrina reported back to Jake and the rest of them. "Oh great! yelled Jake . . . just what Landau wants, some lag time so he can slip away. Has anyone seen Scott or Linda?"

"No, but Bert Jackson just arrived. He just drove in from Zurich and was surprised to hear what the situation is now. I think he's going to talk to the situation commander to advise him about who he is and why he's here. I told him that Jacques Manet is on the way as well. He probably won't get here until late tonight. I hope Helga texted him where he's staying tonight"

"No, it's O.K., I've already sent him a message."

They all approached the hospital, unsure just how close they should be. The police had set up barricades at all the entrances, stopping anyone from entering.

Braco Dragović was sitting in the corner of the room, nursing his wounds when he heard the police arrive at the door to the room. Landau had put up one helluva fight. Two 9mm holes in his chest indicated how he had died . . . his vests had not protected him this time. Braco looked around him, knowing he was at the end of his rope. He had lost his pistol, Landau had managed to trick him into dropping his guard, just enough to allow Landau to get his gun and turn it on him. "Damn!" he thought, "How did that happen? Landau already had two slugs in his chest when he managed to turn the gun around and shoot him."

As he sat in the corner, bleeding profusely, he knew he could not be taken, he could not put Janny at risk . . . his great love Janny. When he heard them out side the door, he knew he had only one option . . . he reached into his pocket for the small vial, his only connection left to Janny. Without any hesitation, he un-corked the vial and swallowed the contents.

The response wasn't at all like he had expected. He suddenly found it was difficult to breathe, but he assumed it was the two slugs Landau had managed to plug into him. His last thoughts were of his beloved Janny, and the fact he had protected her with his last act.

By the time all of the response team entered the room, it was dead quiet . . . in more ways than one. Braco was sitting in one corner, a small vial of poison still in his hand, a peaceful look on his face. Landau was crumpled over to one side of the room, a painful grimace on his face and two very large bullet holes in his chest. It was obvious how the scene had played out, and forensic evidence later backed up their initial conclusions. It was some time before the scene, indeed the entire floor was cleared by the police.

It was much later when Jake and his entire entourage were allowed in. Because both Jacques Manet and Bert Jackson had legal rights to access the scene, they all entered the room as the medical crew were wrapping things up.

"I just wanted to see this son-of-a-bitch" said Jacques, as he looked down on the crumpled body. "When I think about what this guy has done, the lives he has destroyed . . . I almost get sick to my stomach!" He turned to Jake and added "Jake . . . you especially . . . how does this make you feel, seeing this monster like this?"

Jake didn't hesitate. "I cannot feel any satisfaction about this Jacques, only sadness. He had choices . . . he just chose the wrong ones. Things could have been so different . . for many of us."

"So, has anyone identified the guy who managed to catch Landau, and eventually finish him off?"

"Yes, he was Braco Dragović, a Serbian. They're pretty sure he was working for Dr. Dejana Babić, other-wise known as the Serbian Bitch. Forensics and further investigation will tell us more, now that we have him."

"Yes," interrupted one of the medical examiners. You all might be interested to know what he died from."

"What he died from . . . didn't he have a couple of 9mm slugs in him?"

"Yes . . . and that probably would have done him in, but he was in a hurry, didn't want to be caught alive, I think. He swallowed some poison just as the police stormed the door."

"Poison? What poison? How do you know?"

"He had the vial in his hand when they found him, we'll have to check to see what it was."

Jake answered "I think you'll find out that it's a very exotic poison, something you don't normally find in the local drugstore. If you check, I think you'll find it was the same as what they found in Vancouver . . . it's called Batrachotoxin, or some variation thereof. If your chemists have problems, have them call my guy in Vancouver . . . his name is Alan Cook . . . he'd be glad to discuss this with you.

Scott Anderson arrived just soon enough to hear the last news about the poison. "Good God, Jake!, this is almost a repeat of last year, but this time it's only the bad guys getting shot." He suddenly realized what he had said and added "Sorry Jake, I didn't mean to drag up those memories. At least now that bastard Landau is done! Boy . . . this should make a good story as well, almost as good as last year."

Jake answered "But Scott, if my memory serves me right, you were only allowed to write a portion of that story. Will you be able to write this one? We still don't know all the answers."

CHAPTER 44

Both Bert Jackson of the F.B.I. and Jacques Manet of Interpol were stalled in politics and paperwork. Once they had identified themselves to the local command as foreign agents, they were detained for further questioning. After all, they didn't often apprehend two criminals with such numerous international connections, wanted by so many jurisdictions.

They were fascinated with this tall African American F.B.I. Special Agent, and couldn't get enough when he started describing Landau's suspected connections with all of the destructive activities in the U.S. during the previous year, they were fascinated, and of course wanted more detail. After receiving news that Landau had been captured, Bert had come to Austria with plans to extradite him, a plan that didn't seem valid now.

Jacques Manet wasn't any luckier. Although his interrogators were all Austrian or Swiss, and spoke mainly German, they were interested in this obviously very English man with a very French name. Jacques just tried to convince them that that was what the 'Inter' stood for in Interpol . . . International.

If he had seen the trouble that Bert got into, he would have kept his mouth shut, for at least a short time. But curiosity prevailed, and before long he too was taken aside to describe all of Landau's suspected connections with the activities in Europe, including the disastrous 'shoot-out' in Bavaria the previous year.

It was late that evening before they both managed to escape and join Jake and his friends, but only with promises to return the following day.

Jake introduced the two men to the group when they met later for drinks at Scotts's hotel. They all raised their glasses in a toast to the end of their long period of fear and stress. Although Jake never thought of himself as a public speaker, he stood up in front of everyone, leaning heavily on his cane and made a short speech to thank them all, both the two men in the police business, as well as his staff and friends. "I can't tell you how much this means to me. I didn't realize how much the events of last year had impacted me." He paused, looking over to Sabrina with a smile. "But, thanks to all of you, I think I can now move on with my life."

Jake had asked Alan, who had experience as an international traveller, to help Shannon to arrange tickets for his whole office staff to fly out to Zurich and drive to Bregenz. Between his three staff, Sabrina and her family, Helga, and the police presence of Jacques, Bert and some of Sabrina's co-workers, Scott and Linda, they were lucky to all get rooms little hotels and guest-houses in the area.

It was hard to get everyone's attention and conversation away from the subject of Kurt Landau or the Serbian woman. In addition to looking over their shoulders all the time, they were worried that someone was going to either poison them, or kidnap them. As a chemist, Alan was particularly fascinated with the possibility of poison, and wished he could take home a sample of the poison that Braco had swallowed.

Jake tried to divert their attention to their lovely surroundings, so different to what most of them were used to. "Well Shannon, here you are in Europe, Austria to be exact. I said once that we'd get you over here one day. How do you find it so far?" asked Jake.

"I love it Jake, and have to thank you so much for this little perk . . . no, let me correct that . . . this big perk."

"It's the least I can do . . . you guys hold things together in Vancouver while I'm running around Europe."

Shannon looked closely at Jake and said seriously "Jake, I suppose you've given this a little thought, and we've all discussed it on the plane coming over . . . what's next? Are there any more characters lurking around, wanting to get even with you? And what's happening with that Serbian woman?"

Jake started to laugh, "Of course you guys have probably discussed it . . . and you most likely have it all figured out, that's why I love you all so much . . . you're usually one step ahead of me all the time." He paused, then added "But seriously Shannon, I don't know what comes next. To answer your first question, we don't know if there are any more 'characters', as you call them . . . we'll just have to wait and see. And for the second question, so far the authorities do not have any real actionable evidence against that woman, just hearsay and our suspicions. It's going to be even more difficult since she's shut down everything, put everything on hold. We'll have to watch to see if she starts up again, or makes a move. Maybe one day she'll make a mistake. Then, it will be up to Interpol or some other legal authority to make the next step." He paused, thinking to himself that he'd been down this road before. "So we'll just have to wait and see what happens."

- THE END . . . or is it?

9 780228 821311